THE DEVIL'S FOOTSTEPS

From out of the bog alongside the ancient track to the fenland village of Hexney, a line of deep footprints ran, trodden into the dry surface of the abandoned droveway. Each night, the footprints advanced nearer to the village . . . When a young boy's body was found drowned in Peddar's Lode, the villagers' ire was directed at a stranger, Bronwen Powys. The mysterious Dr. Caspian becomes her ally, but they would soon be fighting for their very lives and souls . . .

Books by John Burke
in the Linford Mystery Library:

THE GOLDEN HORNS
THE POISON CUPBOARD
THE DARK GATEWAY
FEAR BY INSTALMENTS
MURDER, MYSTERY AND MAGIC
ONLY THE RUTHLESS CAN PLAY
THE KILL DOG
THE NIGHTMARE WHISPERERS
ECHO OF BARBARA

JOHN BURKE

---◆---

THE DEVIL'S FOOTSTEPS

Complete and Unabridged

LINFORD
Leicester

First published in Great Britain

First Linford Edition
published 2013

A catalogue record for this book is available
from the British Library.

ISBN 978–1–4448–1688–4

Published by
F. A. Thorpe (Publishing)
Anstey, Leicestershire

Set by Words & Graphics Ltd.
Anstey, Leicestershire
Printed and bound in Great Britain by
T. J. International Ltd., Padstow, Cornwall

This book is printed on acid-free paper

When the mighty seven on time's wheel shall spin
The games of the charnel house must begin
Full nigh to that great millennium of doom
When those who went down shall return
from the tomb.
Nostrodamus

The good things are ended; the saints must suffer.
The two-blooded evil one comes, and
begins to prevail.
The Prophecy of Orval

PART ONE

The Spoor

1

In mid-morning the village paused for breath. The parish constable had sauntered his usual unobtrusive path round to the side door of The Griffin and gone inside for his pint of ale. The milk cart clattered down the slope through the old stone arch, horse's hoofs slipping on the cobbles, empty churns clanking together. Autumn sunshine coaxed rosy undertones from the damp plaster of cottages along the west side of the square. A dog barked once and then was silent. There came one of those timeless hushes in which nobody moved in the lanes or square, when conversation in the tap-room languished until someone predictably said, 'Must be an angel flying over,' and even the wind off the sombre unsheltered miles of fenland was stilled.

No angel flew over. But a figure emerged on to the slope below Hexney. It was the figure of a girl, naked, her flesh a hazy whiteness against the grey of the priory ruins. She stepped out across the grass, quickening her pace towards a crumbling buttress. In its shadow waited a darker shadow.

A hundred yards up the hillside Will Jephson watched, unable to look away and unable to move.

Now she was running, but it was an eternity before she reached the crooked finger of the buttress. Will tried to call her name. No sound would come. The scene before him was real, he could swear to it, yet his ankles were trapped in some clinging swamp of nightmare. She ran, her arms spread wide in greeting; but not to him.

She was his wife, who had never showed herself to him like this. His wife, who tormented him with her shyness and prim little voice; who insisted on darkness in their bedroom, reproved him when he tried to coax her into taking off her nightgown in the full glow of the oil lamp, said she loved him but they were married now and folk didn't go on talking about it like that. How could Sarah have become this creature, flaunting herself for the world to see? The world — or just himself and that waiting shadow.

The shadow stepped out to meet her.

It was a dark, stocky man, his skin olive against her paleness, with a swathe of hair running black down his spine from the black helmet of his head. Will Jephson saw only the back of him: thickset shoulders with almost no neck, jutting elbows, swaggering buttocks. He sprang like a goat. Sarah cried out as she was weighted down upon the ground. Her slim legs waved, twisted, and clutched.

His own limbs refused to obey him. His fists clenched but could not strike. Harsh in his throat, his voice could not burst from his lips.

A wisp of cloud drifted across the sun. Shadows trembled. Stones seemed to shift a fraction of an inch and were bathed in a cooler light. Sarah was now only a wraith, and the pulsing dark that had covered her was blotted out by a more intense blackness.

Will's feet escaped. He stumbled down the slope. At last he was able to shout her name over and over again. But when he reached the spot on which the foulness had been played out, only grass and shattered stone sighed under a sudden flurry of awakening wind off the levels.

It must have been a dream. Must, after all, have been a trick of the light.

He didn't believe that.

Sick inside, he turned and hurried home so that he could be there to confront Sarah when she got back.

As he pushed open the door into the stone-flagged kitchen he could hear her singing quietly to herself. She was bending over a pot on the kitchen range, but straightened up to greet him with her usual shy, sidelong smile. She wore her everyday blue and white cotton dress with the cuffs pinned well back, and a dark blue apron. Her face was flushed — from the fire?

He leaned, baffled, against the door-jamb. 'How did you get back so soon?'

'Back?'

'From Priory Hill.'

'But I've not been anywhere near Priory Hill. Haven't set foot outside the house all morning.'

Will looked round the kitchen. It was so normal. And Sarah sounded so truly puzzled. This was all much more real than the wicked vision which had possessed him out there on the grass. Still the scene was vivid in his mind and wouldn't be got rid of.

'Will,' she ventured, 'Whatever's wrong with you, then?'

He went past her into the front parlour. She came after him but stopped, uncertain, in the doorway. Will pressed his brow to the windowpane. There was nobody in sight until Gregory Morritt stumped across the end of the lane. The thickset shoulders jarred Will's memory — the broad back, squat head, lank black hair, dark skin. Gregory's wife had left him, and he had never been one for friends: a solitary drinker, not the kind to joke along with other men. But with that cottage all to himself down along the sluice, there was no telling what he might get up to, no telling about women with more time on their hands than was good for them when their own menfolk were out in the fields or the waterways.

Will swung round. 'What were you up to with Gregory Morritt this morning?'

'Will, What's come over you? I told you, I've not gone a step outside this — '

'Him and you. What's he to you?'

Tears blurred her grey eyes. She put a trembling hand to her lips and shook her head.

The bell in the church tower began to strike. It chimed eleven o'clock in the morning of Saturday the twelfth of September 1885.

★ ★ ★

Three women sat in the spacious porch of St. Etheldreda's preparing for Harvest Festival. In one corner was a stook of barley. Boxes and sacks of peas, beans and fruit had been spread out along the wide stone bench for sorting and assembly within the church.

Mrs. Rylot picked over a box of apples.

'Trust old Sidney to send in all his bruised ones.'

Mrs. Morritt, with a cluster of crocks

and tin vases beside her, snipped ends of chrysanthemum stems with a small knife. After a while she stooped to sharpen it on the step of the porch. When she raised her eyes again, her son Gregory was crossing the square. He caught her gaze, wavered, and looked away.

Mrs. Rylot glanced covertly at Mrs. Lavater. Mrs. Lavater's fingers continued to plait the strands of a corn dolly. They wondered if Mrs. Morritt was going to confide in them.

Mrs. Morritt would not have dreamt of it. She jabbed a few sprays of fern into position behind a cream and gold cluster of blooms, and held the vase out at arm's length to study the effect. They all said she had green fingers. She waited for them to say it again.

'You do have the touch, Hannah.' It was Mrs. Rylot. 'How we'd manage without you I just don't know.'

Mrs. Morritt's lips tightened, as they always did when she had to accept a compliment. 'I do what I can.'

And keep my sadness to myself, she thought.

What had she ever done to deserve such a burden? Other children respected her, and did as they were told. And loved her, a lot of them. This rector and the last one, and the one before that, had all said no one else could ever run a village school as wonderfully as Hannah Morritt. When the boys and girls left, whatever bad things might come to them later in life could never be blamed on Mrs. Morritt. Let anyone say different! Yet her own son, her one and only child, had wantonly turned away from her and let everyone in the neighbourhood see his ingratitude. Perhaps if his father had lived . . . But no, it was no use dwelling on what might have been. The Lord gave and the Lord took away, and the Lord must have meant her to bear this cross. She did not complain. Nobody could ever say she complained or said a word against her boy or against anyone else; she just resigned herself to suffering, tightening her lips against sympathy and against pain.

It was not as though she hadn't wanted him to marry. She had never wanted anything but what was best for him, and would never have stood in his way.

'They say there's a fine lot of eel down past the sluice,' said Mrs. Rylot 'Reckon we'll be getting a few buckets up here by this afternoon. Best decide where to display them.'

It was the nearest she would risk to a sly invitation to talk about Gregory — an invitation, offered by a devious route, taking in the sluice gate and its cottage.

Bad enough that he should have married that shameless Leah.

Nigh on into his forties, going silly over a barmaid, and her already the talk of the village.

And even so I'd have made them welcome. I know my Christian duty, if some don't. Enough room in the house for the three of us, and we could even have managed one or two more if they'd come along. But there he was, couldn't wait to get out. A lot of nonsense, he ought to have been ashamed, about the noise the children made in the school, and all that hymn-singing, and feeling suffocated. As if he was ever there when the children were having lessons. It was *her*. Not much doubt about who put him up to it. All the years he had out of me, and all he could think of was getting out and taking her with him to that hovel down by the sluice.

When I was ill that time . . .

But no, I'm not the complaining sort, I'm not going to cry over what's done with. A mercy there were others only too glad to help.

'Always saying her leg's killing her, but she's not dead yet.' That hussy Leah's voice still echoed. Thinking I couldn't hear her.

Or perhaps I was meant to hear. Nothing you'd put past that creature.

As for the food they served up if you went down there for Sunday dinner — never a Sunday I didn't get the gripes, lying awake all Sunday night. And when I mentioned it, just mentioned it once, not trying to make any trouble between them, what did my own son have to say?

'It's your own add that brings it on, Mam.'

Mrs. Morritt's nose wrinkled above the

funereal smell of chrysanthemums. She looked across the square at The Griffin. Well, the slut was back where she belonged. The only good thing about it, her being back and Gregory not spending so much time in the bar: that was how he had come to be trapped by her, but you wouldn't be likely to find him in there now.

Gregory would come home sooner or later. Sooner or later he would know where he was best off. And his mother would forgive him. It was her duty to forgive.

From the corner of her eye Mrs. Morritt was aware of the old pillory on the green. That was the place for Leah. There was nothing in the Bible that said the wicked should not be punished. Far from it. Some transgressors deserved nothing less than being exposed to their neighbours, pelted with filth . . . flayed alive. Unexpectedly the square began to fill with people. Gregory, about to leave through the gateway, was swept backwards into the centre of the green, which was somehow larger than it had been a few moments ago. The pillory was no longer crumbling and neglected, as Hannah was accustomed to seeing it, but freshly tarred and with two gleaming padlocks. Gregory was jostled towards it.

'No,' cried Hannah; but found she was not uttering a sound. 'No, not him. It was her I meant, that one, not . . . '

The top beam was lifted. Willing hands thrust Gregory's head and wrists into their slots. Down came the wood, and the padlock rattled into place.

Hannah tried in vain to get up from the stone bench.

As if from beside her, from the sacks and boxes and heaps of vegetables in the porch, fruit and turnips and handfuls of earth were hurled into Gregory's face. But they were not the crisp harvest offerings: they were mud, rotted matter, refuse. From every cottage in the square came women with slop buckets, running, laughing. Women: there were very few men at the scene.

Then coat and shirt were torn from Gregory's back. A man appeared, stepping forward and waving the women to stillness. He raised a whip; and began skilfully lashing the hunched spread of flesh, pausing only to flick, every now and then, a few bloodied shreds of skin from the whip. A faint drizzle of warm rain seemed to sting Hannah Morritt's cheek, but when she raised a hand to wipe it away there was nothing there.

The man did not stop until Gregory's back was a scarlet pulp. Then it was all over as suddenly as it had begun. The scene faded, the crowd evaporated. The pillory was once more the decrepit framework fit only for children to climb upon and swing from.

'Just as it was that last time.'

At last Hannah Morritt heard her own voice, escaping.

Mrs. Rylot turned her head enquiringly. 'What was that?'

Dust motes danced in the sunlight. The square was deserted. Mrs. Morritt felt an odd sense of loss rather than horror.

'Thirty years ago it must be. Thirty years since that last time — the last special time, I mean.'

The memory had been so immediate

but was already slipping away. It had not happened. Nothing like this had happened, not then. When? Why should she feel so sure it was going to happen?

'You didn't see anything?' she asked cautiously.

'Only your lad.' Anxious not to appear too prying, Mrs. Lavater looked down; and her busy fingers ceased their work.

'The rector won't fancy that,' said Mrs. Rylot.

Instead of the cross that Mrs. Lavater had set out to make, her corn dolly had somehow turned into a leering demon with a mermaid's tail.

★ ★ ★

Joshua Serpell plodded along the edge of Kobold's Fen towards the village. He was bent almost double, buckled by the ague and rheumatics. Sixty of his seventy-odd winters had been spent in wildfowling, sixty summers in reed-cutting. Today he ought really to have set about rounding up some mates to go on a starling shoot: hundreds of the damned things had descended on the fen this autumn, roosting in the reeds, bending and snapping them so they'd be useless for thatch. But he had something else on his mind. It had to be settled good and sure that he hadn't been drunk or dreaming this last night.

He clambered up the bank to the road, near the level crossing. Hexney Halt was more than a mile from the village. The railway embankment had been built up along the only rodham — firm earth of an old, silted levee — across this stretch of fen. A meandering causeway carried the road to Hexney itself, meeting an ancient drove road at the foot of the island on which the village stood. It was Joshua's well-trodden route to the village and the inn. He had seen Hexney from this angle so many times in his life that he could tell just from the light on it what the weather was likely to be this day and next and a lot more besides. Sometimes the buildings on the tiny hill were as pretty as a picture, especially when the sun softened the flint and brown stone of the church tower, and there was a hint of red-tiled roofs above the wall. Other times, under a pile of clouds sagging down fit to drown the world, it might have been no more than a gnarled lump of bog oak wrested out of the sodden earth, with a spike here, an elbow there, and on that far corner something like an ogre's nose and chin.

Joshua tried to straighten up to take a good look at the prospect this morning. It was getting harder and more painful all the time.

Just beyond the crossing gate stood a young woman in a brown smock with long sleeves, and a kilted skirt. She wore no bonnet but sported deep auburn hair drawn tightly back from her forehead into a gleaming knot above her neck. Her eyes were wide and green. Joshua had observed her a couple of times before, and avoided her, and in particular avoided the glance of those eyes: too much like a cat's for his liking. Today, though, he was going to have a bit of a bother getting past her. She had planted herself and that contraption of hers right in his path.

The contraption was a large mahogany

box camera on a sturdy tripod, with one staring brass-rimmed eye which Joshua found as disturbing as the girl's. He had stood in front of some such thing only once before, in a shop in Ely where he had posed behind his daughter in her wedding group picture, and they had had to keep still so long he had thought his toes would go numb.

What this young woman thought she was up to, lodging with the widow at the crossing and then tramping off all over the place and taking picture after picture, he couldn't imagine. At least they expected you to pay for wedding photographs. No one was likely to pay her for pictures of dykes and churches and tumbledown cottages. One thing, for sure: she wasn't going to squeeze a penny out of him for having his picture taken, if that was her notion.

He edged to one side of the road, above the steeply shelving bank of the dyke. Still she had her eye on him: just like the eye of that gadget of hers, as if they were all set on drawing the soul out of him. Then her attention was distracted. Someone was coming the other way. Joshua recognized the widow's eight-year-old Tommy, trudging back from the fields of stubble. Must have been at it since early morning. Like the other village children, he was off school until gleaning was finished. He had a sack over his shoulder, both his hands were scratched and raw, and he kept his gaze fixed on the road immediately before his feet. As he turned to the wicket gate beside the cottage, the girl called out:

'Tommy.'

The lad came to a stop but hardly raised his head.

'Can you spare me a minute?'

'Well, miss, I dunno. I'm supposed to be — '

'Just one minute. Stand where you are just for a minute, that's all.' As he began to shuffle sideways, she raised her voice. 'I need a foreground figure to give scale to my composition. It really won't take a minute, Tommy.'

He posed reluctantly, a tiny figure distorted into a hunchback by the sack over his shoulder. In the background was the rim of the embankment, and to one side the squat little cottage; still farther on, the hummock of the village sprouted its church tower.

Joshua had no intention of waiting about just in case this young madam picked on him after she had finished with Tommy. There was something not right about her. He felt it in his bones, along with all the other troubles and twinges. Things were building up this autumn that there was no accounting for. What she'd got to do with it he didn't know and he wasn't going to stay to find out. One thing at a time was more than enough. He kept to the edge of the dyke and quickened his pace past her. She was too busy stooping and squinting and sizing up her picture to pay any heed as he reached the gates and crossed the line.

The road made a long loop over the causeway, turning towards Hexney only by the long gash of Peddar's Lode. A faint green scum was forming on the water, and on the far bank of the cut the old punt was pretty well rotted away where it had been left since old Egglington's grandson drowned, that last time.

Last time . . . ? Time for what?

Blades of sedge rasped together, drooping over the murky water. Peddar's Lode looked just as bad under sun as under rain clouds. It was a place you didn't want to get too close to, but couldn't very well steer clear of, the road winding the way it did. Used to be queer stories about it in his grandad's day, and long before that: a place where old heathens, they reckoned, had had a custom of throwing children in to 'feed the fen'.

He reached the drove road, a cleft along the shallow hillside, making its way round the village and across the levels beyond to the rising ground on the Norfolk borders. Half reluctant to learn the worst, he stopped where he had stood last night.

The moonlight had not deceived him. Here were the marks in broad daylight.

He did not dare to bend too close.

From out of the boggy area which swallowed up a section of the ancient track ran a line of deep footprints, trodden into the dry surface of the abandoned drove-way: not old prints solidified in dry mud, but fresh and dusty. Footprints; or hoof-prints; or what? He could not identify them. Roughly triangular, eight or nine inches long, they were set in a nearly direct line one in front of another. Surely not made by any four-legged beast. A man, then, for some reason playing a drunken tightrope game, a wobbly heel-to-toe? But the line was straight and determined and not at all wobbly. And the prints weren't human. To the old fenman's eye they looked like nothing so much as the imprint of a distorted, magnified eel's tail.

Then he realized something — something even more outlandish.

The footsteps had advanced during the night.

There wasn't a doubt about it. He was positive the marks had stopped level with that twisted hawthorn last night. Now they had trodden their way another couple of yards.

Joshua hurried into the village and into The Griffin.

Constable Rylot was firmly planted by

the doorway to the snug, along with two older men and a youngster who dropped in from time to time to collect advertisements and local announcements for the *Wisbech Advertiser*, and who was known to supplement his income by contributing the occasional news paragraph to the paper. They greeted Joshua with nods and a routine mutter of 'Josh' . . . 'Mornin', Josh' . . . 'Well then, well, Josh.'

The barmaid, Leah Morritt called Joshua 'Mr. Serpell'. The landlord, whose wife was safely in the scullery, heating up the copper, took the opportunity of squeezing his bottom past Leah's on his way to get Joshua's old tankard from its hook.

'Hear as they've got a plague of adders under Sowder's Hythe.'

'Been bitten yet, Josh?'

'Wouldn't reckon much on the adder's chance of surviving.'

Joshua drank half a pint without stopping to reply, then began to recount what he had seen last night and this morning. Leah sniggered, and then at a glance from the landlord wilted into sullen silence. 'Great big marks,' Joshua emphasized, 'comin' on, gettin' closer since last night.'

Fortrey, the landlord, leaned on the counter and mopped up a beer spillage and asked the constable very loudly whether there was any news about that poacher who had hidden out here a month ago without anyone getting a sniff of him. Joshua faltered as the men moved away and leaned towards each other over the far end of the bar.

The young Wisbech man said: 'This is interesting. You're really telling us that — '

'I swear to you they're on their way,' said Joshua. 'Them footsteps, they're comin' up the track, comin' up this way.'

Leah was beckoned to fill Joshua's glass. Thus encouraged, Joshua talked across the other conversation. 'If they go on beside the hill and out over the level, maybe that's all right. None of our concern. But if they turn off, like I got the feeling they will do, like turnin' up Tinker's Lane, then they'll be in amongst us.'

Leah winked at the young man. Fortrey

stubbed his right foot against the inner planks of the counter and glared, but not at anybody in particular.

'Go and make yourself comfy in the corner, Josh,' he said, 'and let's hear a bit less.'

'Specially at night, when you're on your way home.' Constable Rylot forced a laugh. 'Happen I'd have to steer you into the lock-up.'

The young man said: 'But aren't you even going to go and see? Isn't it your duty to follow up a report like this?'

There was an uneasy silence, broken by the constable with a thunderous clearing of the throat. 'We know as well as needs be how to manage the affairs of our own parish.'

'I'm certainly going to see for myself.'

'Nobody to stop you, young feller. Us, we know what to take seriously, and what not.'

Joshua had reached the end of his second pint. 'But there's something brewing — '

'And as long as there is, you'd best be content.'

'You know what I'm talking about. Like those times before. Specially that last time, the special one.'

The landlord began noisily to blame Leah for a dirty pot he had just found by the sink, and made a great to-do about mopping the counter yet again. Constable Rylot finished his drink and, with a final admonitory glance around the other occupants of the bar, went out.

'You'll see,' said Joshua.

'And tidy up them bottles while you're at it, girl.'

'It's not just the footsteps. There's a sight more to 'ut than that. Somethin's comin'. Somethin' . . . comin' for all of us.'

When the young man had left to make his own inspection of the footprints, nobody else spoke to Joshua and nobody answered his increasingly aggressive questions. Grumpily he left the inn long before his usual time.

Five days later a boy's dripping corpse was dragged out of the weed and slime of Peddar's Lode.

2

The crossing gates were still open to the road, but a distant feather of smoke showed that a train was on its slow way from Withersey. Visible for miles, it puffed along the embankment above fields and dykes and washlands, for an age seeming to draw no nearer. Bronwen Powys, one arm about her camera so that it did not thump too heavily against the rail of the hired trap, felt like urging haste on the driver. But he knew the roads and the railway and their relative speeds. Allowing for the train's short wait at Hexney Halt, there was plenty of time before Mrs. Dunstall came out to swing the gates across the road.

It had been a rewarding day. Excellent light, fine definition. Bronwen smiled at the inappropriateness of totting up a score on such matters. Yet it had undoubtedly been a worthwhile bag: those almshouses in the shadow of abbey ruins, two wind-mills, and the quite unlooked-for gem of an intricately pargeted cottage. Tomorrow she must tidy up loose ends in Hexney itself, try another study of the church tower and the gateway, and complete another chapter in her self-appointed task.

She shaded her eyes to see how well the scene before her compared with the picture she had taken last week. For a fleeting moment she seemed to see Tommy Dunstall in the foreground, just as she had captured him on her plate. It was a good picture. She must make a print for his mother.

She was about to lower her hand when she noticed something different about the cottage ahead. An assortment of objects had been stacked up outside, like a winter store of wood and peat propped against the wall, since she set out this morning.

They were her own belongings: her trunk, the developing tent, and clothes piled up in a heap.

There was a distant whistle. Smoke from the train streamed away over the levels, at one point wreathing into the swirling plume from a pumping station's blackened chimney.

As the trap slowed between the crossing gates, the door of the cottage opened and Bronwen's maid came out. She was dressed for travelling, her bonnet firmly in place, and carried a bag which she set beside the others. Mrs. Dunstall, close behind, might almost have been bundling her out of doors.

'Oh, Miss Bronwen, there's glad I am you've got here in time.'

'What on earth is happening?'

Mrs. Dunstall's face was blotched by tears. Two men, one with dried duckweed caking his trouser legs and sleeves, stood behind her in the shadow of the doorway.

Bronwen got down and reached into the trap for her camera.

'Don't bring that any closer,' cried Mrs. Dunstall.

'I don't understand. What are all my things doing here, thrown out like this?'

'You'd best be on your way, miss,' said one of the men flatly.

'Mrs. Dunstall — '

'They brought him back. Not an hour ago.'

'Him?'

'My Tommy.'

'Miss Bronwen, I've been packing so we could be on our way, it's all been so dreadful.'

'My Tommy. He was taken.' Mrs. Dunstall's reddened eyes glared terror at the camera. 'In Peddar's Lode.'

'Oh, Mrs. Dunstall, I'm so sorry. I can't believe it. I . . . '

Bronwen was leaning awkwardly, the weight of the tripod on her shoulder, as she turned away from the trap, instinctively putting out a hand to Mrs. Dunstall. The widow let out a screeching sob, warding her off with a wild swing of the arm. 'That thing!' She struck the tripod so that it slid from Bronwen's shoulder. One leg jarred on the flagged path to the door, stuck for a moment in a crack, and then tipped over. There was a crunch as the wood splintered.

'Mrs. Dunstall, you can't believe — '

'I'll not be doing with that in my house. Not after . . . after . . . Should never have had you in the first place, you and that thing of yours. The train'll be here any minute. Be you on it.'

31

'I'm so sorry. Please, if there's anything I can do — '

'You can be on that train, that's what you can do.'

The engine and two coaches drew in to the platform with a sigh of escaping steam. Hexney's one porter and ticket collector stepped forward to open the door of the first-class compartment, a small saloon with four armchairs and a high-backed sofa.

A tall man about thirty years of age, with a silver-topped cane and a cloak lined in red silk, descended and set a large valise on the platform. He had lean features and a swarthy complexion, with darker streaks like bruises under his deep-set eyes, and a jutting imperial beard. When his head jerked to indicate that the porter should pick up his luggage and lead the way out of the station, his manner was that of one accustomed to summoning such service out of thin air.

But the porter had momentarily turned away, signalling to Mrs. Dunstall that she should now open the gates. The fireman leaned out from the footplate to add a similar exhortation.

'I'm not opening the gates,' said Mrs. Dunstall, 'till *she* takes herself and all that evil eye mischief of hers on to that train.'

'You can't expect me to toss everything anyhow into a carriage.' Bronwen was pleading rather than indignant, for she could see that Tommy's mother was near to breaking point. Then she realized that her maid was already climbing aboard the train. 'Eiluned, what do you think you're doing?'

'Do come along, Miss Bronwen. Not safe to stay here a minute longer, is it.'

'Get down at once.'

The girl gulped, but pushed her case ahead of her into the compartment. 'There's sorry I am, miss, but I can't, not another minute indeed.' She groped for the door to pull it shut behind her.

The porter was leaning over the fence.

'Evil eye? Oh, now, Mrs. D, that's no concern of the railway company. We want those gates open, and sharp.'

Instead of obeying, Mrs. Dunstall began to gather up Bronwen's possessions and, sobbing, tipped them over the picket fence on to the road. The porter came through the garden and personally opened the gates. When the train was safely through, carrying away Eiluned but not her mistress, he closed them again, climbed back on the platform, and picked up the newcomer's case.

'This way, sir.'

The driver of the trap sat with the reins loose across his knee, watching with morbid interest the drama between his last fare and the crossing-keeper. His attention was claimed by the rattle of a cane across two spokes of his nearside wheel.

'This will convey me to the Hexney inn?'

The voice was powerful but controlled, with a cadence that suggested singing. Looking the new arrival up and down, the driver assessed the value of his clothes and general appearance and the probable tip. 'If you could hold on just a jiffy, sir, till this young lady settles what she owes.'

The man glanced at Bronwen, struggling to save her effects from further damage. 'It would seem highly probable that the lady will require your services further. I suggest we offer what assistance we may in conveying her, also, to Hexney.'

'Oh, now, sir, I'm not so sure about that. Not with all this fuss. Best let me get you to the inn, and then we'll see — '

'I can already see. The lady is in distress. If she wishes our help, she must have it.'

Bronwen held out her arms in a last imploring gesture to Mrs. Dunstall, then let them fall to her sides. The two men who had been shuffling awkwardly in the background now plucked up courage to leave, sidling past Bronwen with their faces averted and trudging away towards Hexney. Mrs. Dunstall went indoors. Curtains had been drawn across all the little windows.

The stranger said: 'You'll need time to collect your thoughts as well as your impedimenta, madam. I shall be privileged if you will accompany us to the village.' It was said with sonorous determination, as much for the driver's benefit as for hers.

35

She prickled with instinctive, inexplicable antagonism. The man was too sure of himself and, in spite of his politeness, too threatening. She did not understand the threat; but did not approve of the way the driver, abandoning any further attempt at argument, sprang down as nimbly as a performing dog and began to collect up her belongings; she was also conscious of a further confusion to add to the distress she was already in — a blurred vision of that red-lined cloak spread wide like the wings of a swooping bat. It was ludicrous, yet briefly, overpoweringly vivid.

He was saying: 'If I may help you up, Miss . . . ?'

'Powys,' she said stiffly. 'Bronwen Powys.'

There was really nothing for it. The cottage had become tragically hostile, there was no shelter on the vast expanse of fen, there would not be another train until after dark, and that would deposit her for the night in an unfamiliar city; and in any case she did not see why she should be forced to decamp before her work was complete. Perhaps tomorrow, or just before leaving, she could venture to offer Mrs. Dunstall condolences and soothe her fevered imaginings. Meanwhile she had no alternative but to seek accommodation in the village.

The man's fingers were strong and supple under her elbow as he assisted her into the trap.

'Thank you, sir.'

'Caspian,' he said. 'Dr. Alexander Caspian.'

'Yes,' she said. Then she was puzzled by her own immediate response. The name had come as no surprise, though she could swear she had never heard it before.

He was quick to catch her reaction. 'You know of me?'

'No,' she said. 'No, I'm afraid I don't.'

'For a moment I thought . . . ' His eyes mocked her. For some arrogant reason he suspected her of being familiar with his name.

Why should she be?

They settled on the narrow seats at opposite sides of the higgledy-piggledy heap of luggage and Dr. Caspian frankly and appreciatively studied Bronwen's face.

She had to say something. 'It was most kind of you to come to my assistance.'

'You don't belong in these parts.'

'They make that very plain.'

'A foreigner. In the English countryside we are all foreigners unless we have been here for ten generations.' It occurred to her that he was in every sense a foreigner. His English was beautifully modulated, but there was something alien about him. 'But that scene,' he went on, 'appeared unusually violent.'

'It seems I'm regarded as a witch.'

His regard seemed to burn more and more deeply into her. She was sure her cheeks were flushed, perhaps smeared with dirt from trying to cope with clothes and cases dropped on the earth, and that her hair must have been blown and dragged this way and that.

Lingering softly on each word, he said: 'It is difficult to blame them.'

★　★　★

From the bumpy road Hexney gave the impression of a small fortified town rather

38

than a mere village. The place had grown up around a makeshift castle with a bailey but no keep, overlooking bare expanses of fen plagued by Saxon outlaws and keeping the Norman defenders' feet dry. It was still ringed by a medieval wall, punctured now by gaps through which lanes and a back road had been driven. The widest opening was straddled by a Norman gateway with two drum towers too substantial for the dumpy little hill. From a distance the church tower was a pinnacled landmark. The closer one approached, the farther out of true the tower seemed because of its bulging stair turret.

The trap clopped and grated its way up the last steep slope and in through the gateway.

Bronwen had already surveyed every inch of what lay within. The wall was merely a shell, protecting a village green that had been mutilated to make way for a cobbled marketplace. On one side The Griffin bore witness to a more prosperous past. Through its imposing frontage a beamed entrance led to a stable yard, and the depth of the main building promised more accommodation than would be needed today. Railways had robbed the posting houses of their splendour, and such new roads as came into being were many miles away, making wide circuits to the Wash and the east coast. The inn was not so much derelict as shrunken; like the whole village, huddled in on itself.

The trap stopped. The driver jumped down and stood to one side as Dr. Caspian helped Bronwen down. Then he cleared his throat.

'You won't be forgetting, miss . . . ?'

Bronwen opened her reticule and settled her day's account. Caspian nodded peremptorily at the luggage and left the man to deal with it as he escorted Bronwen into the inn.

Through an open door drifted the smell of polish and scrubbed tiles, and the clinging sourness of ale. A fire burned in the grate in the hall. Beside it was an alcove filled by a large bureau, its drawers and pigeonholes raggedly stuffed with papers. The landlord, hearing wheels rattle over the cobbles, had already stationed himself by it with one proprietorial hand on the open flap.

'My name is Caspian. Dr. Alexander Caspian. I telegraphed for a room to be reserved.'

'That's right, Doctor. Quite in order, sir.'

'And I'd be obliged if you'd provide this young lady with accommodation. She will let you know in due course how long she intends to stay.'

'Well, now. I don't rightly know about that, sir. We wasn't expecting . . . '

'You're not telling me your establishment is full?'

'No, Doctor. But after what's happened, after what I've been hearing only this last thirty minutes or so, I'm none too sure how my regulars would take it . . . '

His excuses petered out as he caught the full hot blast of Dr. Caspian's gaze.

Bronwen stole a glance at her protector. The bone structure of that saturnine face, the smooth darkness of the skin, gave it a positively Slav cast. Deep furrows on each side of his nose emphasized the flare of the nostrils. When he spoke, the throb of his tone and the accompanying insistence of his eyes, as ebon as a mountain tarn, seemed almost to mesmerize his audience.

Audience . . . ? She groped for the thought, and it was gone.

'Whatever you have heard, mine host, can assuredly be no more than contemptible tittle-tattle. In a profession such as yours, hearing what you must hear in your own bar day after day, I imagine you know how little substance there is in outpourings of that nature.'

'It's not me, sir. Not at all. My regulars . . . '

'Your regulars will desert you only when by some stroke of fate their thirst deserts them.'

Bronwen said quietly: 'Dr. Caspian, having so newly arrived upon the scene, I think you cannot know the full story.'

'And do not need to at this moment. When I do hear it, I am confident I shall prefer your version to any other.'

The landlord rested his weight on the flap of the bureau, which creaked a protest. Abruptly he forced a smile. It was meant to be ingratiating, but the muscles of his face tugged downwards as if against his will.

'Right you are, sir. Don't see why we shouldn't fit the young lady in.'

Caspian nodded, having taken it for granted that he would get his way. But Bronwen sensed another strange element in the landlord's swift surrender — a kind of nudge, given to the man by some force he himself didn't understand, something elusive which seemed about to come into focus but then retreated.

She rubbed her hand across her eyes. Perhaps she would have done better to let herself be bundled unceremoniously on to that train.

'If you'll come this way, miss, I'll show you to your room and get Mrs Fortrey to see you've got all you need.'

The room had a low ceiling with blackened, sagging timbers, and a latticed window overlooking the square. The carpet was worn thin along one edge, and the coverlet on the bed was badly faded; but it was clean and unpretentious, and Bronwen welcomed it as a temporary refuge. A young man brought up her cases, the large camera and her portable dark-tent, stacking them along one wall. He was followed by Mrs. Fortrey, who eyed this paraphernalia dubiously.

'A towel for you, miss. And I'll get the girl to fill the washstand jug when she comes in from the scullery.'

'Thank you.' Bronwen wanted only to be left alone, to sink into the armchair by the window and recover her scattered and mangled wits.

'There won't be any ... well, you won't be splashing acids and things? On our carpets, I mean, miss.'

Bronwen tersely reassured her. She had no intention of throwing acid about. But perhaps, instead of sitting down, she ought to open up her boxes and see what, if anything, had been damaged as the distraught crossing-keeper threw them out of doors and over the fence.

Mrs. Fortrey went to the door, expressing one last disquiet. 'You've got no maid with you, then, miss?'

'She took herself off. A most unreliable girl. She'll have no reference from me, that I can promise.'

Mrs. Fortrey raised an eyebrow, evidently sympathizing with the girl rather than her deserted mistress, and left.

Bronwen carefully opened out the folds of cloth around the dark-tent box. Nothing appeared to be leaking. She raised the lid to find one bottle dislodged from its compartment but mercifully undamaged. She had less luck in her plate storage box. Two glass plates of the Church had been cracked diagonally. The scenes would certainly have to be taken again. And here she would stay until they and several others were perfected, ignorant savages or no ignorant savages.

She turned her attention to the camera tripod. The injured leg was the result of the iron ferrule driving up into the wood. Any weight on it would widen the crack.

When water had been brought and she had washed and tidied herself, Bronwen went downstairs. There was nobody about, but she did not trouble to ring the handbell on the bureau. After so many explorations of the village she remembered her way round well enough.

It took only a few minutes to find the carpenter's shop in West Lane. The sagging fence and the gate yawing on its hinges were no great advertisement for the craftsmanship of the occupant; but from the shed came the pleasing tang of newly sawn wood, and through the gaps in the planking she saw the gleam of yellow deal.

An elderly man within was completing work on a coffin.

When Bronwen pulled the door back he looked up and froze, then began to tap the end of his screwdriver on the lid.

'I wonder if you could repair a camera tripod for me? One of the legs has split.'

'That has?' A shrug, a shake of the head. 'Got my hands full right now.'

'I don't believe it would take long. Even if you could manage only a temporary repair, to keep me going while I'm here, it would be a help.'

He lowered his gaze and contemplated the coffin. 'I'm likely to be asked for another one. Got to get this finished, and then there's the talk of me having to do another one this next couple of days.' His head went on one side, sly and accusing.

'If it isn't repaired,' Bronwen persisted, 'my work here will take me a lot longer.'

That seemed to strike home. 'Well, I'd have to see it first.'

'I'll bring it round. I do assure you, it's a fairly simple job.'

'That do depend.'

'If I go back and fetch it now — '

'Leave it till tomorrow art'noon, then.' He beat out a slow tattoo on the woodwork.

She left before he could change his mind. The light on the church, as she crossed the square, was just right for a picture. Now was as good a time as any to attempt a replacement of those cracked plates and at the same time to check that the camera itself was undamaged. She paced round the edge of the green in search of the best vantage point, and a solid base for the camera.

Of course. The lower platform of the pillory. The camera would need only the slightest tilting to take in the whole church tower, and the rising lens devised by her father would prevent vertical distortion. Bronwen went back into The Griffin and fetched the bulky box and cloth of her portable darkroom. When she had propped it against the pillory she went back again for the camera, glancing twice from her window to make sure that nobody was meddling with the equipment on the green.

In the hall as she came down this time, Dr. Caspian was talking to the barmaid, a plump girl with milky complexion and lips gone slightly sour — lips which now pouted and promised, under the spell of the slim, tall man and his extravagant presence.

'Them footsteps, sir? Well, they do wholly puzzle every one of us. But we reckon it's best to say nothing and let 'em go away.'

'You can tell me exactly where I may observe this manifestation, Leah?'

He spoke her name as if he had been speaking it intimately for years. She swayed enticingly towards him and giggled. 'Fancy someone coming all this way from London just because of old Josh Serpell's maunderings!' She edged herself closer to Caspian and, at the door, took his arm and leaned her left breast against him. 'Your best way, sir' — her face was turned up to his — 'is turn left outside here . . . if you could wait till later . . . wanted me to show you the way . . . '

Bronwen swept past them and across the cobbles and grass to the pillory.

She balanced the camera carefully and established that she could achieve quite an agreeable composition. Satisfied on this score, she set up the equipment box on its stand, shook out the folds of lightproof cloth, and slid aside the flap of the red-tinted window. Wriggling under the cloth until it was draped over her head and shoulders and down to her hips, she prepared the collodion coating for a plate, and then transferred the plate-holder to the camera. Again she ducked under a cloth, and groped forward to adjust the focus.

Upside down, hanging beside the church tower like a bat hanging by its feet, Dr. Caspian swam into view with one hand on his cane, the other raised to doff his hat. Bromwen was about to shout and wave him aside. But the plate was ready. Dr. Caspian's exaggerated pose before the tower was as good a test piece as any, and she wanted to waste no more time. She pressed the bulb.

As she took the exposed plate quickly back to the tent, Caspian observed: 'A somewhat outmoded technique, surely? I understood the day of the wet plate was past.'

'Dry plates do not produce results of the same quality. Useful when one is moving about, but not for serious studies. My father refused ever to work with them.'

'Ah. I am told Charles Lutwidge Dodgson recently gave up photography altogether for similar reasons.'

'Besides,' said Bronwen, plunging back into her dark-tent, 'one can check one's results in a matter of minutes.'

Most important if you could not be sure of returning to a site to rectify mistakes. And once she had left this surly place she doubted if she would wish ever to return.

Carefully she poured on the solution of acetic and pyrogallic acid, and slid the plate into its hypo bath. Now, as on so many occasions since his death, she could almost believe that her father was still at her shoulder fussing, squeezing in under the cloth or grunting a 'Hm, hm' outside, and a 'You'll lose it if you don't look lively', or at most a 'Well, I've seen worse, mm, yes'.

The picture clarified. She was glad her father was not there to see the final result. The tower was as she would have wished it, Dr. Caspian emerged strong and clear, just as he himself would have commanded it. But between him and the tower, a peculiar shadow swirled and thickened, darkening into a cap above the darkness of his head. It was vexing. And more than that. Even in the negative form, where white was black and black was white, she was disturbed by the grimace of that faceless shape behind Caspian's shoulder — something warped and violent, some hint of predatory lips and menacing talons.

'You let some light in,' her father would have chided her. 'Isn't that it, mm? Or someone crossed the green and you didn't even notice.'

Meredith Powys had been a Caernarvon architect who discovered early in the experimental days of photography the advantages of showing prints of existing buildings to his clients when explaining his own plans. He also, for his own satisfaction, amassed a collection of pictures of his native Wales, and in due course ventured across the borders. Unlike so many of his contemporaries he was horrified by the demolition which went on in the name of industrial progress: several years before alert preservationists created the Society for Photographing the Relics of Old London, he was hard at work recording threatened buildings for posterity. If a row of old cottages or some corner of an abandoned castle was marked down for destruction to make room for a new railway or a new factory, it became the custom to call in Meredith Powys so that at least a two-dimensional memory of its existence might be preserved.

Mrs. Powys presented him with seven daughters. Two died in infancy, one went to America and was never heard of again, three married — two living still in Wales, one in London. Bronwen was the youngest. Sixteen when her mother died, she had looked after her father's depleted household and helped him with his work. Most of his time in later years was devoted to photography, and most of that time was spent away from home: the grey stone house in Caernarvon was too hollow and too haunted. He sought the past, travelling, making notes, obsessively taking pictures of churches and abbeys, of great houses and straggling hamlets. Bronwen went with him. She sorted out his notes, kept his files and records, catalogued the accumulation of plates, and coaxed him homewards again when their load grew too bulky and it was necessary to devote some weeks to slotting glass negatives into their appropriate places in the library at Caernarvon.

For some time before his death it had been tacitly accepted as inevitable that Bronwen should continue his work. Once there had been talk of her becoming a teacher until such time as she married, but nothing had come of it. 'Time you left me to it, girl,' her father had said on a number of occasions. 'Time you thought of yourself.' Or, 'Don't have to be hanging round me all your life, now, Bron.' But he would have been devastated if she had taken him at his word; and what pleased him most and mellowed his last painful months was her assurance that his collection would continue to grow even when he was no longer there.

The echoing hollowness of the slate and granite house was even more desolating after he, too, had left. His executors, the local solicitor and a second cousin from Llanberis, assumed Bronwen would sell it. Instead, she extended the library into a second room, and converted two of the ground floor rooms into a commercial photographic studio. It was a somewhat daring venture for a young unmarried woman with no male guardian on the premises but her family had been known and respected for so long, and she was so affectionately established in local minds as 'Meredith Powys's ginger one', that allowances were made for her. Wedding groups and a certain amount of fashionable portraiture for the gentry brought in a fair income to supplement what her father had bequeathed her; but she did not neglect that other inheritance, her task of expanding topographical and architectural records as her father would have wished. Several weeks each year were set aside for exploration and accumulation. Usually they were uneventful weeks. She would find some inexpensive place to stay, take her pictures, make the relevant notes, and depart. It was rare to encounter trouble such as she had unwittingly run into at Hexney.

Nor were her troubles, apparently, over. The camera must have suffered some damage. How else could that strange blur have insinuated itself by Dr. Caspian's head, writhing down out of the sky? Back in her room, Bronwen tilted the plate to and fro between her palms. It was not that Caspian himself had moved: his outline was perfectly sharp.

It was too late to make a positive print in this fading light. She would have to wait until tomorrow.

★ ★ ★

From her window she saw Dr. Caspian emerge from a side lane into the village square. He was sunk in thought, his head down, his cane tapping a steady rhythm across the cobbles. She was able to look directly down upon the top of his high-crowned hat as he entered the inn.

He was already seated in the dining room, a decanter on the table before him, when she went down to eat. As she entered the room he stood up.

'Good evening, Miss Powys. Will you take wine with me?'

She hesitated.

'The landlord's cellar contains no great treasures, but I have unearthed a more than tolerable claret which must have crept in without his noticing it.'

A place had been laid at another table, closer to the fireplace; but it did seem rather absurd that the two of them should conventionally keep their distance in this large, unpopulated room.

'That's most kind of you.' She sat down.

'I trust the results of your labours were satisfactory?'

'Not altogether. Something went wrong.'

He went to the other table to fetch a second glass and, returning with it, poured glowing red wine and set it before her. 'I have a suspicion I was at fault. I made some foolish gesture when I should have remained rigid.'

'I'm sure it wasn't your fault. There must have been some trick of the light. It produced a very strange shape at your shoulder, Dr. Caspian.'

He raised his glass to her. His eyes gleamed as deep and dark as the wine. 'Don't tell me you have been concocting spirit photographs? You really must let me into your technical secrets. They could prove most useful in my own profession.'

'I'm still ignorant of what that is.'

Instead of taking her up on this he said: 'If you could spare me half an hour of your time, I believe you might be of some service to me here, tomorrow.'

'After bungling one picture of you — '

'I wasn't thinking of my own image. What I need are some photographs of the footprints.'

Mrs. Fortrey, fussing up to the table, stopped short. Then in a strained tone she said: 'I laid a table for you over there, miss. Thought you'd find it more cosy.'

'I have invited Miss Powys to dine with me,' said Caspian, 'and she has graciously accepted.'

Mrs. Fortrey looked at neither of them but at a spot in mid-air somewhere above their heads. 'Very good, sir. I'll re-set a place here. Will soup and lamb cutlets suit both of you?'

As there was no implication of any alternative being available, Caspian and Bronwen agreed that soup and lamb cutlets would suit admirably. It was not until Mrs. Fortrey had left the room that Bronwen took up the subject again.

'The footprints?' she prompted.

'Yes. The footprints. You know of them, of course.'

'I've heard some conflicting stories. Or, rather, fragments of stories.'

'You've been to inspect them yourself?'

'Naturally I went to see what the rumours were about.'

'How many times?'

'Just once.'

'Then you have not verified whether or not they are advancing?'

She regretted having been drawn into discussion of this subject, and resented his inquisitorial manner. 'It's not the most direct route into the village,' she said lamely. 'And I have been occupied in other parts this week — Thorney, and Croyland.'

He nodded. His scepticism was all too apparent. Again she bustled. She had no intention of revealing to him the unease those marks had aroused in her, or her reluctance to go near them again. They were none of her business; and her feelings and conduct were none of his.

Really, she ought not to have sat so readily at his table. When he invited her it had not occurred to him that she would refuse. How much more might he take for granted?

Two dishes of rich vegetable soup, each a meal in itself, were set before them. As

Mrs. Fortrey moved off, obviously eavesdropping for as long as she could manage it, Caspian set out with calculated loudness to question Bronwen about her work and about modern cameras and printing methods. She found herself expatiating on the aesthetic superiority of calotype over the admittedly more manageable emulsion plates now commercially manufactured, on albumen and carbon prints, and on possible substitutes for fragile glass negatives. He drew her out — truly he was mesmeric when he chose — on the niceties of naturalistic photography, tinted portraits, *cartes-de-visite*, and stereoscopy; and listened with flattering attentiveness to her own preferences in equipment and processing.

He was particularly interested in techniques of double exposure, but when she thought to use this as an opportunity for turning the conversation towards his own occupation, she discovered how late it was. The meal had been ended for some time, and she caught herself about to yawn, her eyes stinging with tiredness and the upsets of the day. Caspian had suavely directed the conversation along her own line of interests, and revealed nothing of himself.

As they were about to leave the dining room he said: 'I may count on you, then, tomorrow morning? What time would best suit you for taking photographs of the footprints?'

'Dr. Caspian, you have given me no hint of your reasons for interest in this matter. I've told you a great deal about my own work. So far I know nothing of yours.'

'I'm a magician.'

'Seriously, I mean.'

'Most seriously I mean,' he said, 'that I am a magician.'

3

A shaft of sunlight broke free from the long shadow of the village wall, striking brightness from a thousand drops of dew still trembling on cobwebs in the shade. Autumn haze receded slowly and patchily across far fields and dykes. As the sun gained strength, the ground itself seemed to glow. Shadows oozed out and away from the firmly impressed footprints.

The shape of each impression was clear and undamaged. There should be no trouble with identification. Yet trouble there undoubtedly was: Bronwen, standing beside Dr. Caspian as he knelt beside a print to measure it, jotting a few figures in his notebook, had never seen any foot or hoof remotely resembling the outline. Each sunken imprint was eight or nine inches long and roughly triangular, splayed rather than rigidly three-sided, with the apex at what might be regarded as the heel. There were fine ridges in the dust such as one might see along a fish's tail; but as the print expanded forwards it looked more like a webbed foot than a tail.

Fruitless to try conjuring up a picture of some hypothetical creature capable, like the mythical sciapod, of hopping along on one webbed foot. And just as puzzling to interpret the motives of any trickster coming here at night to contrive such prints in the driveway: a devious prank.

'And' — Caspian straightened up — 'they *have* moved in the night.' He indicated a blaze cut into the overhanging branch of a bush eight or more feet away; and a white line chipped down a stone on the other side of the track. 'I made those marks on my first inspection yesterday.'

'The stone could have been shifted.'

'But not the bush. Not without leaving some trace.'

He stood with head bent, contemplating the line of footsteps marching up from the fen and heading inexorably . . . to what destination?

This morning he wore a short chesterfield with a shoulder cape its collar faced in dark purple silk. It made him look curiously enclosed, his wrists emerging as separate entities without disturbing the hang of the cape. His head was bare, and when he bent forward there was an eerie white streak across his crown of dark hair as sleek as a badger's snout.

He watched, with some show of deference, as Bronwen set up her camera Without the tripod, she had to try the strength of various bushes, until at last she found a stunted tree with two branches forming a firm, useful crook. They would have to wait, though, until the sun came fully over the bastion some yards up the slope.

Bronwen said: 'You really came all this way to inspect these prints?'

'I did.'

'But how did you hear about them?'

'The *Morning Post* picked up a few paragraphs from some local newspaper hereabouts. The tale they told bore a remarkable resemblance to something which happened years ago, in another part of the country — something,' said Caspian remotely, 'for which I have always wanted an explanation.'

A troubling intimation drifted across her mind as ephemerally as one of those glistening cobwebs, shredding between branches caught in a faint breeze. She caught a tug of fear from the back of his mind, so direct that she stared at his lips, half expecting them to be still moving, confiding in her. But his lips were closed, his eyes lowered.

How could she have heard, when he had not spoken?

He was taking a leather wallet from an inner pocket. Inside were three neatly folded newspaper cuttings. He unfolded them in turn and passed them to her. While she waited for the light to come full down on the droveway, Bronwen read the yellowing columns.

Two issues of *The Times* had printed tongue-in-cheek reports, flippant in spite of authentication by scores of witnesses, of a strange happening on the night of the eighth and ninth of February 1855. There had been a heavy snowfall in Devon, and during the hours of darkness a trail was left across that snow — a trail more than a hundred miles long. Footprints wove a path in and out of villages through Totnes to Littleham, and actually crossed the ice-bound river. The crisply preserved spoor was that of a cloven hoof, but not the hoof of any identifiable animal. The regularity of the prints, each some eight inches ahead of its predecessor, suggested a two-legged rather than a four-legged creature. Unfaltering, they went on through gardens and closed gates . . .

Bronwen turned over the cuttings. The third was from *The Illustrated London News,* in which a correspondent gave details of his own observations:

'This mysterious visitor generally only passed once down or across each garden or courtyard, and did so in nearly all of the houses in many parts of several towns, as also in the farms scattered about. The track passed in some instances over the roofs of houses and haystacks and very high walls (one fourteen feet) without displacing the snow on either side, passing on as if the wall had not been.'

'And there were other letters,' said Caspian. 'Full of suggestions as to the identity of this traveller.'

Bronwen shook her head. What nocturnal hunter could have raced so far at such a pace, brooking no obstacles?

'Half-frozen birds!' Caspian went on scornfully. 'That was one theory. But birds don't leave the impression of a hoof, and birds wouldn't drop on the snow in one direct line. An outsize rat in search of food . . . an otter . . . and one zoologist claimed it was a kangaroo. A kangaroo — at large in Devon on a winter's night?'

She handed back the cuttings.

'I have others in my collection,' he said. 'One from Heidelberg about intermittent appearances of just such marks in Galicia. And a correspondent in Holland has referred me to reports on something that trod the Dutch polders during the skating season ten years ago. Farmers and fishermen there had the same theory as our own superstitious countryfolk: they called the marks the Devil's Footsteps.'

'And *your* theory?'

'So far I have none. If it were possible

to establish some cycle . . . ' Caspian turned once more to the droveway. 'Why are these tracks moving so slowly? In Devon, a hundred miles in a night. Here, no more than a few yards.'

'It is purely scientific interest, then, that brings you to Hexney?'

His hesitation was barely perceptible. 'Scientific interest,' he said.

Sunlight dazzled through a gap and laid a bright swathe down the path. Bronwen leaned against the tree and inched her camera into position. She made two exposures, then Caspian asked if there was a way of getting closer and recording the prints from different angles, to provide an approximation of three dimensions for study. With his help she steadied the camera in the low cleft of a sapling, then risked balancing it on a small pile of rubble fallen from the wall. He followed her orders and manifested the subdued respect of one skilled craftsman for another — whatever his own craft might be.

When they had finished, she promised to see if prints could be prepared for him by this afternoon.

'If our worthy landlady doesn't burst into your darkroom with accusations of witchcraft!'

He shouldered the cumbersome apparatus, but instead of taking the shortest route back into the village set off at a comfortable stride along the droveway, pacing on from where the footprints left off.

The old track made a wavering arc round the outskirts of the village, parallel with the wall, and then veered off across the fen and more distant marshland. Five miles on, more solid ground sloped up to the county border, and an avenue of beech trees marked what was probably the continuation of the drove road. Were those slowly advancing footsteps going to trudge on across the flat miles and then climb the slopes and make for the far coast? Or would they choose a spot at which to swerve inwards, into the village itself? Just possibly the whole thing might fade out as inexplicably as it had started.

They paused at the junction with a well-worn track up to a breach in the wall. Obviously this would link up with the lane down which they had left the square a little while ago. Bronwen said:

'We can go in that way and relieve you of all that weight.'

But Caspian, unheeding, was sniffing the air. A freshening wind brought a sour yet cloying tang with it. It was not the fetid smell one might expect from stagnant ditches or rotting vegetation on the levels, but something working and fermenting near at hand. Caspian went on a few paces to where the wall turned north.

Bronwen had been here before and knew the sight that presented itself to him. The ramshackle buildings were little more substantial than beehives. There was a peat-walled shack with a millwheel under its thatched roof, immobile now. Ranged below the village walls were skeletal sheds with long racks and flimsy shelves of hazel twigs. From other sheds, enclosed against the light, came the smell, which had already stung their noses and palates, together with a faint splash of water and a mutter of voices. As Caspian led the way past this shabby little industrial offshoot, a man with a kerchief fastened across his mouth came out, untied a knot, and breathed in air which, contaminated as it might be, was obviously preferable to what he had been enduring in the darkness.

Caspian waited for Bronwen to fall into step with him.

'So there is at least some occupation for the men of the village.'

'Woad,' she said.

'Still surviving? In spite of all the new dyes, the new processes?'

'It seems to belong, somehow.'

He looked at the decrepit mill and couching sheds, and nodded wry agreement.

'I do think,' said Bronwen, 'you ought to shed that load.'

This time he gave in and turned up beside drying racks towards another entrance through the wall. It admitted them straight into the lane beside the church.

A few yards within the lych-gate a small, freshly dug grave yawned damp and raw between settled stones and rectangles of gravel.

They stopped, and looked up the churchyard path.

Names repeated themselves in family clusters. Rylot, Morritt, Serpell, Lavater — and, flanking the open grave, any number of Dunstalls. The community of the dead was as tightly knit as that of the living.

Set apart from the others were a few isolated stones which one felt had been allowed in only on sufferance. A mere two or three Fortreys, Bronwen noticed. There was one on its own which was hard to read from this distance. She leaned on the wall and narrowed her eyes, trying to make out the lettering. Fovargue: surely alien?

'One of the few contributions of new blood in many centuries,' said a voice behind them. 'And it did not run in local veins for long.'

A plump man in dark clerical attire, with a high white collar, had followed them up the lane from the rectory and was studying them with slightly apprehensive courtesy.

'A Brabant refugee.' He waved a limp

hand at the solitary stone. 'There were several such during the persecutions of the seventeenth century. But few of their line survived here. After a while they tended to leave and settle elsewhere. It's an inward-looking place.' The hand flapped round towards them. 'I am rector of this parish. Wint. Sebastian Wint.'

They shook hands and introduced themselves, and Caspian said:

'Yes, one does get the impression that your flock is slow to accept newcomers. And' — his gaze strayed to the new grave — 'quick to seek scapegoats.'

The rector's gaze was nervous, seeking out Bronwen and then dodging her. 'A tragic mishap. Tragic. One would dearly like to know . . . ' He shuffled to the gate and held it open. 'You have seen the interior of our church?'

They followed him up the path. Caspian set the camera on the stone bench in the porch, and they went on into the cool interior.

The church was well cared for but bleak. Dampness had clawed a few green inches up most of the nave columns. On

Bronwen's right as she walked beside Caspian up the aisle was a succession of fairly conventional poppy-heads at the ends of pews. But when she glanced at the bench ends to his left, she observed some oddly contorted figurines. Their bestial features had aroused several questions in her mind when she first examined the church, soon after arriving in Hexney; but before she could ask about them, the rector said:

'We're rather proud of our pulpit. Very fine Jacobean work, an excellent specimen.'

It was indeed a splendid three-decker with pulpit, lectern and clerk's seat: another relic of the village's lost affluence.

Along the wall of the south aisle was a dark blue curtain. With a jokingly conspiratorial wink the rector drew it aside to reveal a medieval Doom. The colours had faded from the woodwork, but still preserved an ironic distinction between the saved and the damned: the women among the latter were plumper, pinker and prettier, and even on their way to hellfire looked more cheerful than the pious, pallid wraiths of those ascending to heaven.

'We keep the curtain drawn most of the time,' explained the rector. 'Wouldn't want to distract the congregation during morning service, mm?'

Some of the choir stalls were surprisingly ornate for such a remote place. Bronwen waited for Caspian's reaction as he lifted a seat, to be confronted by an obscenely grinning demon in one of the misericords — not the skittish imp one so often found introduced by jovial local wood-carvers, but a thick-lipped monster with lolling tongue and lewd eyes. The next one was no better. The third portrayed, as far as one could make out, the upthrust buttocks of some bawdily exaggerated beast.

'Er, yes,' said Wint. 'Those must have been brought here from the priory, after the Dissolution.'

It was a strange source for such perversities. Idly Caspian lifted another seat, to find something newer and less durable. A corn dolly wedged into a gap in the woodwork was swinging its head up and down with the rise and fall of the seat. Modern though it was, it had a devilish head belonging to the same family as the carvings; and when he tugged it out and extended it for Bronwen's inspection, it proved to have the tail of a fish — or a merman.

The church was not merely cool, but cold. She shivered.

The splay of the tail and the ribbing of the corn stalks reminded her of the footprints outside the village.

'A remnant of our Harvest Festival,' said the rector uneasily. 'Last Sunday.'

'Rather pagan for a Christian festival, wouldn't you say?'

'It's . . . um . . . one of those local quirks. One grows accustomed.'

The dry dolly squeaked between Caspian's fingers. Bronwen had a sudden prevision of him rushing to the church door and hurling the object out into the fresh air. But the impulse was suppressed. He remained where he was, motionless save for the scrape of his fingers round the plaited throat.

'I tend to turn a blind eye,' said the

rector, 'until the Gathering is over.'

'The Gathering?'

'A harvest supper on Saturday. Tomorrow.'

'Isn't it usual,' said Caspian, 'to have that on the Saturday *before* Harvest Festival?'

They proceeded down the north aisle and came to a halt beside the poor-box, a brass-bound oaken chest with a slot which was no mere slit in the lid but a pursed, inviting mouth. Wint said:

'Elsewhere, yes. In this part of the Black Fens nothing is usual. It is said of Hexney folk that they are forever looking over their shoulders. We may regard it as only too typical that for them the great celebrations are in the reverse order — and the reverse order of importance, I grieve to say. After years as local shepherd I have to confess I find my flock has . . . how shall I put it . . . ?'

'Cloven hoofs?' With the rector off balance, Caspian pressed the point home. 'On that subject, sir, what do you make of the prints on the drove road?'

'Nothing, sir. I make nothing of them.'

'You've given them serious consideration?'

'I did chance to come across them when visiting a sick parishioner.'

'And your conclusions?'

'Another local freak.' The rector observed that his visitor was still carrying the wicked corn dolly, and took it from him, laying it in the corner of a pew — if not reverently, at least with wary respect. 'Some twisted cross-breeding out of the washlands, perhaps. I am not a zoologist, but — well, one gets strange inter-marryings of species, you know. Not all the legends are crude superstition. Unlike the village' — he tried another of his uneasy chuckles — 'where they don't care to marry outsiders.'

'A water-borne freak?' said Caspian. 'Crawling out at night and then picking its way backwards each morning in its own footsteps?'

'Oh, I admit there are inconsistencies. Oddities.' The rector was holding the heavy door open, inviting them to leave. 'I tend to see the whole thing as symbolic.'

'In heaven's name, of what?'

'Not in heaven's name, I fear.' The

rector struggled to look knowledgeable and infinitely tolerant. 'They have their own ways here, which I fear you will not have the time to understand. Their own idea of what constitutes humour — and reverence. I find it best not to meddle. I do what I can, in my own way. And that's enough.'

'Is it?'

'No,' said the rector painfully. 'No, it's not. But it's all I'm capable of. I'm no miracle-worker.'

'It only takes application,' said Caspian.

* * *

Bronwen carried her tripod to the joiner's yard and extracted a grudging promise from him. Using the churchyard wall as a prop for her camera she was able to take some pictures of the square and its cottages, and spent the rest of the afternoon sketching out a programme of remaining subjects to be tackled before she left.

In the early evening she was on her way into the inn, past the open door of the taproom, when it seemed as though someone had spoken directly to her and forced her to stop — someone close to her ear, though the men wrangling together were on the far side of the room.

'The evil eye, ain't nothing else to call it.'

'No you can't put that on her, that's not how it is.'

'No more that ain't.'

'I tell you — '

'You know's well 's I do what's comin' . . . '

Then they saw her and were hushed. Yet in the silence they went on mutely talking: she could still hear them. As she forced herself to move on towards the stairs, the words chased after her.

What's comin' . . . The echo within her head swelled to a choral incantation. *Shaping up . . . ready for the coming, as it was and shall be . . . and once it's started and there's no getting out . . .*

She tried to relax in her room and make a few notes. The buzz from the taproom would not allow it. Words and phrases were no longer distinguishable but she found herself straining to hear — tense to catch things that were not even being said.

When she came down to eat, the taproom was empty, and in the dining room only one place had been set. She dined alone. Caspian's absence produced in her a mixture of relief and a disappointment to which she did not care to own.

It was late when she persuaded herself to forsake the large room and the fireside and go to bed. She could not explain her own reluctance to turn away from the sputtering, hospitable flames.

She had her foot on the bottom tread of the staircase when Caspian came in. He was lost in thought, preparing to pass her as if she did not exist.

Then he paused beside her.

'Goodnight, Miss Powys.'

His intonation came as an almost physical shock. They stood apart, yet she had the tingling sensation of his touching her. While his eyes skimmed her throat his fingertips were virtually stroking her flesh. He stared, as started as she was; then looked away as if to deny her reaction and his own; and now it was as if his hand were slowly and sensuously relinquishing her arm.

She hurried upstairs away from such impertinence, breaking the contact.

Was it in his power to restore it when he chose?

Bronwen washed in cold water from the jug, then pulled back the bedroom curtain to reveal a cloud-streaked sky. The window rattled once, twice, experimenting and then deciding she was not to be disturbed. Faint laughter throbbed downstairs and died away into a mumble. A few men must have returned to the bar and were staying late; or perhaps Fortrey and his insolent-eyed barmaid were tidying up.

There was a faint smell of lavender on the sheets of her bed. She lay on her side. watching wisps and hillocks of cloud merge and reassemble.

Somewhere in the hotel Dr. Caspian was thinking about her. Instinctively she framed an answer, then jerked herself over on her other side and thrust him away. She felt him recede; felt him moving a long way, steadily, going further away than she had anticipated.

His voice and others bowed themselves out of her mind.

It was not the first time she had been jolted by such an experience. Rarely had it been so clear and immediate. Conditions in Hexney seemed to sharpen the faculties. What had once been fitful and unintelligible was beginning to come through as if a muffling curtain had been drawn aside to allow direct, insistent communication.

Once it's started and there's no getting out . . .

She turned over in bed a dozen times and still could not sleep

The night was growing colder. The bedclothes were heavy on her, but a chill seeped in from all sides. It was ridiculous. It must be a dream. A short time back she had been, if anything, too hot as she tossed to and fro. Now she drew her knees up and pulled sheet and blankets as close to her throat as possible.

Caspian was calling her.

Of course it had to be a dream.

She was shivering. When her tremors ceased it was not because of warmth returning but because of an even more terrible, numbing cold. She tried to push herself upright. It was death, and not sleep or dream, which would claim her if she did not escape.

She could not move.

Caspian's voice crackled away into icy despair.

Panic-stricken, Bronwen made a last effort and kicked the bedclothes away. She forced herself to fall out of bed.

The cold drained away. Dazed, she stumbled to the window and looked out. The square was frozen under a sky faintly luminous with a scattering of stars. Houses shifted a few sly inches when she was not staring straight at them: neglected for an instant, they settled into older shapes, their modem plaster crumpling around an original framework. Rotting thatch above a dormer window took on the shape of a bushy, quizzical eyebrow.

All at once the aching cold returned, biting into her ankles. She heard agony.

Heard, not felt it. Heard Caspian's torment jangling into her head along cruel slivers of ice.

If she did not go at once it would be too late.

She fumbled into skirt and blouse, coat and shoes. The ache began to crack her mind apart but she drove herself quietly downstairs through the sleeping hotel, groped for the bolts, and let herself out into the night. It was mild and still. She knew that, though every screaming nerve denied it.

Caspian's call was dying away, but still was clear enough to guide her. She broke into a run, down the lane and out through the wall, stumbling on to the ruts of the drove road. Too late she thought that she should have brought a lantern. Through a lattice of leaves she glimpsed the dancing glow of a will-of-the-wisp above a long drainage channel. Dank mist swirled bitterly around her head; yet there was no mist — no mist, no breeze, no sound, nothing but the paralysis of death cramping the limbs.

In the uncertain light she picked out

darker ruts a few paces ahead. They were the footprints that Caspian must have come out to study, hoping to catch some hoaxer at his senseless games — or to catch whatever else might be at large.

But there was no sign of Caspian.

Fear grew colder than the icy strangulation. Had that mental summons been part of a terrible charade, the exercise of some dark power, which she had sensed earlier but fatally failed to understand?

She found him in a huddle behind a bush, sitting cross-legged with his hands on his thighs, patiently staring at the track. She knew he was aware of her and was trying to raise his head; but the movement was beyond him.

'Get up,' she said loudly. 'You must get up.'

Something cried out to her. He was still there, he was still just within reach.

'Up,' she cried. 'You must get up on your feet.'

She put her hands under his armpits. He tried to speak without words, and she caught at his will and held on to it and dragged him towards her. His right leg moved in excruciating pain. His foot braced itself against the ground and he lurched upwards. She took his weight against her shoulder.

'Walk,' she commanded. Were the shadows gathering to bar their path? 'Walk. This way.'

Mentally she urged his steps to match hers. They trod slowly along the drove-way, and it was not until they were close to the wall that she dared to look back and see if the footsteps were pursuing.

The night was innocent. The footprints were little more than blurs in the half-dark. She could not tell whether they had advanced during the night; and certainly not whether they had advanced a few paces while her back was turned.

The chill was ebbing away.

'How did you reach me?'

The sound was no longer only in her head. Caspian rasped the words out as he stopped, eased his aching shoulders, and stood away from her.

'What happened to you?' she demanded. 'What could have stricken you down like that?'

'I . . . what made you come looking for me?'

'I heard you crying for help.'

'I had no chance to cry out. And from that distance, from the inn, how could you — '

'I heard you,' she said simply. 'From within your mind I heard you. And I came to you.'

4

Bronwen Powys was the seventh daughter of a seventh daughter.

Her grandmother in Wales had been credited with the gift of second sight, though this had never been authenticated by any truly significant prophecy. Bronwen's mother had been taken by fey moods but learned to subdue them. Mr. Powys would countenance no such nonsense. Sometimes he joked his wife affectionately out of her fantasies, sometimes was stern and peremptory. As for Bronwen, he permitted not even the vestige of a dismissive joke. When she was five she had once brought him a pencil without being asked, and when he wondered how she could have guessed he was just about to look for it she explained: 'I heard you wanting it'. He grew immediately forbidding. She must not play tricks, must not misinterpret coincidences, must not listen too readily to her grandmother or to what other folk hinted about her grandmother. Many a time after that she caught fleeting strands of her mother's thoughts, and an occasional wisp from somebody else, like a garbled cry from a horseman galloping past and not waiting to repeat himself. Partly from innate obedience to her father and partly from her own inability to evaluate the meaning of these experiences, she shied away from them — deliberately turning, as it were, a deaf inner ear.

Other children seemed to go through a similar phase when they were little, within their own families, but grew out of it. Bronwen did not grow out of it. When her father was left a widower and they began to work so closely together she found herself anticipating scores of his demands before he had fully formulated them, and without her consciously applying this faculty of hers or fully understanding what it was. She concealed its existence as one would conceal a private, embarrassing ailment from even the most cherished friends and acquaintances.

There had been a young man in Caernarvon, handsome young Evan Williams, who was yearned after by all the well-to-do farmers' daughters and the slate quarry manager's daughter. Evan wanted none of them: he wanted Bronwen Powys. It was generally considered a match that no sensible girl could turn down. Yet the idea of marrying Evan was untenable. He had looks, he had money, he would make a kind husband and probably a good father. Her reasons for rejecting him could not be explained to her friends or to Evan himself, or to her own father. In point of fact Mr. Powys did not demand much in the way of explanation, being well content that she should continue to live at home and work with him.

How could she convey to anyone her awareness of the emptiness, the lack of a dimension, within Evan Williams? There were no words to describe what was lacking. A simple everyday phrase came closest to describing what she meant: within that handsome exterior there was nobody at home.

If she was to be satisfied, there must be a certain resonance. She had not heard it yet but was sure she would know it when it sounded. Somewhere, some day, it would strike; or, if that was not to be, then she could do worse than to live the rest of her life alone.

Never before had anything so penetrating as that silent call from Alexander Caspian reached her. He had the power, as she herself had it: she recognized it, as she had always known she would recognize it. But it was not what she sought. Could not be. The resonances were harsh and discordant. She sought harmony and, ultimately, unison; not discord.

'I don't hear you,' she had once vainly said to the baffled Evan Williams, who after such a wayward remark was perhaps glad she had refused him. Now, after close and alarming communion with Alexander Caspian, she found herself being treated with mistrust because she *had* heard.

Across the breakfast table in The Griffin Caspian said: 'I'm most grateful to you for coming to my rescue. But you haven't explained exactly what alerted you.'

'I tried to tell you on our way back.'

'I was not at my most receptive then. And I fancy you, too, were a trifle confused.'

'On the contrary. I was very wide awake.'

'There were one or two fancies about mind reading — spirit messages — which I can't credit. Possibly I misheard.'

'Not spirit messages,' said Bronwen: 'a direct personal message from your own living mind.'

'Oh, dear. Oh, dear me.' Caspian sounded infinitely condescending. He waited until Mrs. Fortrey had set plates of bacon, egg and kidneys in front of them, and then added: 'If you read my thoughts so clearly last night, can you read them now?'

Bronwen stared into his eyes, but their glowing challenge made it impossible for her to concentrate. Yet when she looked away, the contact was even more tenuous.

'You are not allowing me to do so,' she

said. 'You had no barriers up last night. This morning you will not let yourself be heard.'

Caspian's lip curled. 'A crank by the name of Myers coined a word a few years ago to describe what you're postulating. Telepathy, he called it: the transmission of concepts from one mind to another without the use of recognized sensory channels.'

'Why should you dismiss him as a crank?'

'I have made it my business to investigate many such claims. None of them stand up. I cannot accept the possibility of psychic substitutes for those normal sensory channels.'

'Cannot — or will not? After what happened last night? I do assure you — '

'We can all store up impressions on a level of the mind below normal consciousness.' Caspian cut into his fried egg and watched the trickle of yolk across a rasher of bacon. 'I think it feasible that, without realizing it at the time, you heard me leave the hotel and guessed where I would be going. The thought fretted you,

94

kept you awake, until in that state of half-dreaming you were impelled to come out in search of me.' The patronizing manner infuriated Bronwen. She burst out: You're accusing me of — '

'Miss Powys, please. I should be the last person to accuse you of anything. I'm deeply in your debt. All I'm saying is that in your case I believe that what we call the subconscious mind made some decisions for you of which you were not consciously aware.'

'And the cold? That icy cold — you won't deny that you felt that?'

'Some localized freak. Some natural phenomenon: a cold patch due to some flaw in the subterranean water table, a drift of mist from one of the dykes trapped in some tree and bush formation . . . something of that sort.'

'Rubbish,' said Bronwen, with her mouth full. She chewed desperately. 'You're talking yourself away from the truth. You're hiding something. Why?'

She sensed a pang of alarm on some far horizon of his mind, instantly suppressed.

'A less romantic concept than you

favour — is that what upsets you?' He kept it very steady. 'But then, reality is very unromantic.'

'Hiding something,' she repeated, pushing her chair back and standing up.

'You're leaving without trying this delicious conserve?'

'I find you insufferable.'

'Oh, Miss Powys, I've already told you how glad I was to be rescued by you last night. Whatever the cause of your errand of mercy, you saved me from some unpleasant agues.'

'That's all you think you would have suffered?'

He said firmly: 'I cannot accept that any other elements could have been involved.'

She turned on her heel and left the room, feeling angry and foolish and perturbed all at one and the same time.

★　★　★

The coffin was lifted from the carrier's cart, shrouded in black crape for the occasion, and carried up the path to the porch. The mourners, a few in shiny black suits but most in working clothes with black armbands, fidgeted at the gate and then moved in twos and threes to join the villagers already seated inside.

Bronwen, in the back pew beside a cold stone column, saw heads begin to turn towards her.

She lowered her eyes.

There was a hush. A foot scraped on the pulpit steps, and then again there was an unnatural stillness.

She looked up. Necks were still craned round; eyes condemned her; it was hard to believe that anyone was breathing. The Reverend Sebastian Wint blinked an unhappy, unspoken appeal down at her.

Nothing would start so long as she sat here. Tommy would lie there in his coffin, beneath the array of wreaths, until he rotted and until the flowers withered all away, if she did not leave. Bronwen felt her palms grow sticky within her dark gloves. They all accused her. All commanded her to leave.

Except one. There was a young man — somehow she knew his name was Will Jephson — who sat beside his wife and stared straight ahead, beside his wife yet far removed from her, indifferent to the church and the funeral service that ought to have begun, thinking vaguely but obsessively of a tangle of naked limbs, thinking *Tonight . . . then we'll see . . . the Gathering . . .*

Still the rector was waiting upon her going. Trying, perhaps, to summon up the courage to come and ask her outright to leave. He dared not begin with her still in the church.

She would have despised him if he had not been so pitiful. High principle was too much to ask of such a man.

Bronwen edged out of the pew and left the church.

In the callous sunshine, sadness hung on the air. Soon Tommy Dunstall would be lowered into that gash of clay. Tears and sullen hatred would impregnate the ground and the very stones of the village; Tommy's name would be on everyone's lips, memories would haunt them — for how long? For a few hours, she thought, until those selfsame hypocrites who had mutely banished her from their ceremony would find their voices again in the drunken, bucolic good cheer of tonight's ceremony, the Gathering.

It was a hateful place.

Worse than that. Terrible. The word scorched into her mind. *Terrible is this place.*

Spurned by church and congregation, she was tempted to flounce into The Griffin, pay her bill, and ask the time of the first train from Hexney to anywhere, absolutely anywhere. But that was just what they would have wished. She would go when it was clear that the going was her own choice. Her work would be finished; she would leave; and would be delighted never to return.

The taproom was being subjected to an especially thorough scrubbing this morning. The funeral service ended, more men than usual would be in here. And presumably there would be even more tonight.

The inn felt dead. Or, at least, in a state of suspended animation. She heard, sensed, nobody. Caspian had gone out soon after breakfast, that she knew. He had tried to hire the trap, but the carter had said he was busy with more serious matters — the funeral, undoubtedly — and could not oblige. Finally Caspian had hired a nag from him and ridden off looking somewhat grotesque, a fine figure of a man on a sagging and sluggish animal.

She collected camera and tripod, hung the plate-box in its satchel over her left shoulder, and, giving the church a wide berth, went down to the priory ruins.

There must once have been a substantial boundary wall, but stones had been fetched from it to build houses in the village and repair the churchyard wall; and grass had grown over the littered remains. The only solid remnant of this girdle clung to a buttressed, fortified gatehouse.

Bronwen had taken one picture of the gatehouse from the outside. Now the light was right for another study from within.

The priory, according to her researches before she came here, had been founded in the eleventh century by one of Norman William's barons, a patron of the Cluniac order. Its ravaged church looked picturesque from the west, perilous from the east. Settling of the unstable ground had tipped some pillars of the bare nave out of true, at the east end tilting one towards another, at the west threatening to splay out and let the arcaded tiers of the western façade collapse between them. Beside the church were fragmented cloisters and a well-preserved chapter house, refectory and infirmary building, chequered with knapped flint.

Bronwen took two pictures of the prior's lodging, one from a distance and one close enough to bring out the intricacy of the flushwork on its south wall. In a gap between the lodging and the infirmary wall was a stone outcropping, which falsified the geometry of the main buildings. It was an anchorite's cell, in which perhaps some devout man or woman once lived out a sequestered life and was walled up after death. Three gargoyles on the skeletal roof above snarled and grimaced down: rather than warding off evil spirits they appeared to be luring their fellows to come and do battle with them.

In search of further subjects, she

stepped over rubble in the opening of what had once been the west door of the priory church. The arch above her head was flaking away into a chalky smear, but half-eroded traces of lettering could still be distinguished in the stone:

TERRIBILIS EST LOCUS ISTE

'Terrible is this place,' she murmured aloud.

Cold shadow scudded across the grass.

A young man sauntered along the top of the slope. The funeral service must be over, folk were drifting away.

And the thoughts of Will Jephson, on his roundabout way to the inn while his wife went home, drifted and settled, drifted off again.

Sauce for the goose, sauce for the gander.

It died away like a thin echo trailing off down a long valley.

Bronwen stood in the shade and tried to hear the truth, tried to dismiss the critical whisper of Dr. Alexander Caspian's doubts. How much, he was asking, had she really caught of a disturbance in that young man's mind, and how much was she inventing? How much was a product of her own imagination — a misinterpretation, given misleading significance by some trick of what Caspian loftily called her own subconscious mind?

I heard him, she said to herself under the grey shoulder of a dissolving pillar: his name is Will Jephson and I heard him and I don't know what it means and I don't know what he was talking about in church this morning or what he was talking about when he passed a few seconds ago but I heard him.

There was no way of holding these moments of revelation in focus. They happened erratically, uncontrollably, in fits and starts and invariably when she was not in a mood for concentration. If she tried to grasp the essence of the message, it at once flew away. But its squawk and its fear, or its menace, were nonetheless as real as the flutter of its escape.

Knowing that intense, deliberate concentration achieved nothing, she supported herself with one hand against the jagged stone and tried to follow Will Jephson.

He had looked round the pews in the church and seen that Mrs. Morritt was there, having the time of her life as the rector read about death and they all sang about death. He also noted that Gregory Morritt was not there. Beside him, Sarah tipped her chin back and stared at the cracked angel in the roof. Even when most of the congregation had turned to glare the foreigner, the young madam who had put her curse on Tommy, out of the building, Sarah had remained pale and unmoving. She knew Gregory Morritt wasn't there. And no doubt she knew where he really was, and they had arranged something. Certainly they must have something arranged for the Gathering.

When they left the church and stood for a while at the graveside to watch the little coffin being lowered in, he had a moment of dizziness, as if he was going to pitch forward and fall in himself.

Oughtn't Tommy to have been left in Peddar's Lode? Hadn't he been put there to complete that corner, and didn't it spoil things for him to be lifted out and laid somewhere else?

Or was the sacrifice itself enough?

Will rubbed his eyes, bewildered.

Sarah said stiffly: 'Well, then. I suppose you'll want ten minutes with the rest of them. But don't be late for your dinner.'

He watched her go. But he was not going to join the rest of them. Not yet. While the men made for the inn, he walked slowly round the square. Twice round. Each time he passed the open window of the taproom he glanced in. Smoke swirled out, heads were close together. He caught a glimpse of Leah Morritt's fair head. A trollop. Everybody knew that. But he wondered if she was all they said she was — all of them laughing and telling coarse jokes about her, but enjoying her. 'Trollop,' he said fiercely between his teeth.

He left the square and went past the church, down and out of the village and along the slope by the ruins. That mad young woman was working away down there with her box and bits. If she had not been there, would he have seen Sarah again . . . and Gregory Morritt?

Sauce for the goose, sauce for the gander.

Twice he had followed Gregory Morritt, trying to catch him meeting Sarah. And once, instead of going off to the far end of Grimm's Dyke where he was supposed to be working, he had kept an eye on his own house waiting for Sarah to come out and hurry off. They were too cunning for him. But he had seen them once; they'd be at it again, sooner or later.

Perhaps tonight.

He reached home, and let himself in very quietly.

Sarah started back from the range. 'You gave me a proper turn.'

The stockpot was on the fire. Sarah had been smearing something on slivers of bread and tucking them inside the larder door. He saw them before she closed the door. As she ran her hands under the tap and reached for a cake of green soap, he said:

'What's all that, then?'

'Rats have been getting in, under the door.'

He drew a deep, shuddering breath. 'What witch got that stuff for you?'

'Oh, Will, you're not in one of your moods again?' She drew a chair back from the table and indicated that he should sit down. 'Everything's ready. I'll not be a minute.'

'You think I'll just sit down and let you fill me with poison?'

She tried to laugh. 'Oh, come on, my cooking's not as bad as that.'

'I'm not eating here today.'

She was getting stubborn, he saw. A few days ago his attempts to trip her into telling the truth had brought tears to her eyes. Now she went very white, but there was a hard set to her lips. Proud of herself and what she was doing, that's what she was.

'Will, do you sit down and let's have an end to this nonsense.'

'I'm not eating here.'

He stumped out. He had not caught her out yet, but he would.

Was it safe to turn his back on her?

Men were moving away from The Griffin. A small cart stood outside from which an eel-catcher was unloading buckets of eels ready for the Gathering. Will nodded to him and went into the taproom.

It was almost empty. One surprise, though: he had been looking for Gregory Morritt, and here Gregory was, leaning on the far end of the bar counter and looking mighty uncomfortable. He had been drinking alone as usual, away from the others, and all of a sudden must have found there were no others: they had all gone home to eat. So there was just himself and his wife.

Leah was mopping the bar, well away from him.

'Well, how're you keeping, then?' Gregory said awkwardly, just as Will entered. The remark had been meant for Leah, but Gregory turned it thankfully on Will. 'That's time for a drink, I reckon.'

Will wasn't going to take a drink from the likes of Gregory Morritt. He had half a mind to turn and go out. But he had wanted to know where Gregory was, he couldn't deny it. And here he was. And as long as he stayed here . . .

Leah was smiling at him. Smiling to make it quite clear that he was welcome and Gregory wasn't.

'Hello, Willy.'

She had never called him that before, and never used that tone of voice to him. It sounded husky, as if it was going to crack down the middle any minute. And she was leaning her breasts on the bar, and her lips weren't thin and disapproving like Sarah's but full and inviting.

'You're late.'

He might have been one of her steady customers, one of her most dependable regulars.

Gregory shuffled, and banged a toecap against the bar rail.

'What will it be, then?'

Leah had to move halfway back towards her husband to draw the pint of ale. He rattled coins as if about to pay for Will's drink, but Will clapped the money down on the counter. He watched the way Leah walked, and the way her bare arm swung as she set the pot down. Trollop, he said to himself. It ought to have made him feel disgust, but it was having the opposite effect. A woman who'd give herself. They said she had given to plenty already. Not to Will Jephson.

He stared and she knew he was staring and she was enjoying it.

Gregory Morritt made a noise in his throat which meant nothing to either of them, and the grunt he made halfway across the taproom might have been a sort of goodbye; but although Leah knew he was going she gave no sign.

Again she was leaning on the counter. 'Well, then.'

* * *

Bronwen crossed the threshold, the load on her right shoulder blotting out the view into the taproom. But she knew there were two of them in there, and knew that one was the young man who had crossed her line of vision above the priory.

He laughed, and the barmaid laughed.

Beneath their laughter she heard the same thought from both of them, strong because simultaneous.

When that night comes . . .

Something was building up, assembling factors, solidifying, bound together by a passion, a commitment — building up or perhaps more accurately boiling up. Ready to overflow, she thought, at tonight's harvest Gathering for which the whole village waited.

5

Eel stew bubbled in a cauldron over an open fire on the grass. In the early dusk, gouts of smoke spurted out as new branches were driven into the fire, drifting away in dark wisps against the ashen sky, broken by streaks of light the colour of pale embers. A few youngsters mimicked a witches' dance around the cauldron, then fell uneasily silent and strolled away to the edges of the green.

Fortrey and Leah Morritt were laying out tankards along a trestle table outside The Griffin. Three large casks had been racked up close to the inn wall, and two brawny young roadmen taken on as extra barmen waited with their sleeves rolled up.

The lanes and cottages buzzed and rustled as girls studied themselves in looking-glasses and giggled about the phantom lover who might look over their shoulder.

Reverend Sebastian Wint drew the rectory curtains tightly shut and settled down with a bottle of port and a volume of Archdeacon Farrar's lectures.

Gregory Morritt, with one foot on his mother's brightly scrubbed doorstep, said: 'You want to come along tonight, Mam?'

'To that disgusting rout? You know me better than that.'

'I just thought you might want to come, if I was along with you.'

'Oho. And what's all this about, pray?'

'I was just asking if — '

'You don't want me to come.'

'Would I be here now if I didn't?'

She was angrier than she had been when he was not even speaking to her. His coming here like this threatened, somehow, to upset things. Now that she had made her mind up . . . Not knowing what she had made it up about, she said tartly: 'You've only come because you felt you ought to. Not because you wanted to.'

'But Mam, if I didn't ask, you'd go on about for not asking. And when I do ask, well, you — '

'I know when I'm not wanted,' said Mrs. Morritt.

'Well, don't you be saying I didn't ask.'

He went off towards the square.

They were all congregating now: girls arm in arm venturing out from the lanes, some boisterous lads toiling up the hills and in through the gateway, some older folk in decorous little knots at the corners of the green. Dusk became as smoky as the fire. As a flame licked up, shadows clawed away towards the far wall, and a twisted silhouette of the pillory was sketched on the cobbles.

Bronwen leaned on the windowsill of her room and looked down.

She had not known exactly what to expect, but felt it ought to have been something fraught with more meaning than this. There was no maypole, no hay wain, no bustling master of the revels, no lord of the manor unbending and benevolently scattering largesse to his farmers and their hands. So far the Gathering looked like being little more than a limp survival of some older more vigorous festival.

Eels were being ladled out into bowls. Men edged sheepishly away from their wives towards the beer table. Gregory Morritt had his hands planted on one end, jabbing his head at his wife as he talked pleadingly, insistently. Leah, almost directly beneath Bronwen's window, shook her head. Gregory went on, as if afraid that the clamour of the growing crowd would drown him out once and for all if he did not make his point now.

'Come on, girl,' growled Fortrey.

Leah turned away from Gregory.

A row of torches was driven into the grass near the pillory. In their fitful light the face of Hannah Morritt, standing back close to the church, was a throbbing red glow. Someone in a darker corner began to sing a dirge, largely on one dismal note, until laughter and a splash of oaths rolled over it.

Hannah Morritt stared across the square and followed her son with her gaze, followed him into the shadows and still did not altogether lose him.

Gregory Morritt will be punished.

The message was as clear in Bronwen's

mind as if it had been delivered full into her face, at the top of the messenger's voice. Then, like the dirge, which had begun a few minutes ago, it was engulfed in a surge of other impressions. Scattered voices and thoughts were beginning to join in a more powerful whole. A mere spectator at her window, she felt the tug of an insistent rhythm below, pulling her down. Different groups were amalgamating: not purposeful yet, but awaiting the declaration of some purpose. Strollers around the perimeter adopted a steadier pace, and at the heart of the square a dozen girls began to circulate in the opposite direction. Here four, there six, older people stood like squads waiting to be ordered into action in a military tattoo.

The pattern was broken by Mrs. Rylot, stumbling across the cobbles in an odd, crouching, erratic gait.

'My Winkin. My cat.' People laughed, stood apart to let her through, closed ranks again. 'I'm sure I locked him in, I *know* I did.'

She peered into crannies, stooped again to chase shadows between people's feet.

'Puss, puss . . . ' Bronwen's faculty of inner hearing had never been so sharp as since she came to Hexney. And was at its sharpest when worked by a certain catalyst. She was forced to recognize it, while resenting it. At this moment it was not just the combined forces of the throng below, which dragged at her, but something else. She knew Dr. Caspian must be back from his ride.

She looked towards the gateway, knowing that he must come through it.

He rode in, slowing to avoid the mounting excitement of the outer ring of walkers, now transforming themselves into dancers. In the spluttering flame and smoke she had a picture of him, again, with his cloak spread, of beating wings, of some demonic master of the revels.

But that was not how the revellers saw him. The path they made as he moved forward was not to welcome him but to be rid of him as soon as possible. He was alien, he marred the rhythm of the Gathering.

As they all glowered their dismissal at him, the screech of an animal in torment rose from the far fringe of the crowd. A man snatched up a torch, but its smoke only added to the uncertainty. Then, over the heads of the girls whose slow circling of the green had been broken, a contorted dark shape was tossed towards the cauldron. For a moment in the light it was not dark but dripping red. Then it splashed into the stew, and those closest backed away from the spatter of scalding liquid.

The woman who had been serving out eel plunged her ladle into the cauldron, fished for a moment, and lifted it out with a shapeless mess draped across it.

Mrs. Rylot shrieked in an agony as hideous as the animal's.

From where she leaned on the sill, Bronwen could see unmistakably what the object was: a flayed and bloody cat.

She retched, and turned away from the window. Protest and horror beat over and into her head. But the horror was not at the sight itself or at Mrs. Rylot's grief: it was at something out of sequence, something as disruptive as the presence of Alexander Caspian.

Too soon . . . not tonight, not this time . . . too soon.

Mrs. Morritt, wiping her hands on a tuft of grass pulled from the green, came beside Mrs. Rylot and put a hand on her arm.

'There now, my dear. Loss comes to all of us. It's all been decided, it is all foreseen, there's nothing to be sad about.'

Gregory Morritt, too, must be punished.

As he rode below the window on his way to the stable yard, Caspian looked up at Bronwen's window. Even without turning her head she knew that he was looking for her.

She knew she had to go down.

Slowly she descended the stairs, hearing the noise beginning to swell again and beginning to flow into the hall through the open door.

When she set foot outside, the throng parted, as it had parted for Caspian. She hesitated, not knowing which way to go. She was no part of it, she wanted to be no part of it; and she was not waiting for Caspian — she did not know what she was waiting for.

Fortrey twisted the tap of the cider barrel and jerked his head at Leah. 'Go round and collect some o' them mugs, else there'll be no more drink for some of 'em.'

Leah pushed a strand of hair back from her gleaming forehead and began a circuit of the green.

Well back from the firelight, his shoulders against a flinty wall, Will Jephson waited for her. When she was within his reach his hand touched her arm and ran up it to the hot stickiness of her throat.

'It can't be now,' she said.

'It starts now,' he said. 'Did you know it was going to start?'

She stooped to pick up a tankard, and held still for a few seconds so that he might stare down through flickering darkness into the deeper darkness of her unlaced bodice.

'Old Fortrey'll be shouting his head off if I don't get some of these back to him.'

Her fingers clamped through the handles, clanking the pots together. Will held her by a fistful of skirt while he took something from his pocket. It was the ferret-fur tipper he had taken this evening from his wife's drawer. Given to Sarah on their engagement, it was lined with silk and padded with sheep's wool. In one end had been a snippet of Will's pubic hair, in the other of Sarah's. For making happiness and making children. It hadn't worked. Now one end was empty: he had unpicked it and thrown away his wife's hair.

'You'll fill this,' he said, 'and give it back to me on the night.'

He dropped it between Leah's breasts. She laughed and wriggled, as if to settle it more comfortably, and swung away to scoop up three more tankards between her arms and hurry them back to the table.

Some unmarried girls — four, then five, then six — were separating themselves from the inner ring and forming a new circle of their own. They began to dance, chanting verses that sounded too childish for girls of their age:

'Ring around the green,
Bones and bones I've seen:

One, two, three, four,
Burn 'em up below the floor.

One we'll do the jig,
Two we'll lose the pig.
Ring around the green
Say you haven't seen.'

The dancing quickened then slowed into a solemn swing of heads and shoulders and pale young arms.

'Keep it from your throat,
Give it to the goat . . . '

Bronwen saw Caspian emerging from the yard, under the blackened oak beam of the entrance. Silently she said to him because she had to have someone to talk to, that it all sounded like some local variation on Ring-a-ring-o'-roses. And he answered, without picking her out of the crowd, something offhanded about a scapegoat sacrificial chant. Did he even know that it was she who had spoken, she to whom he was responding?

The girls were swooning and swaying

from side to side. An acrid note invaded their singing, and the dance was corrupted from an innocent tripping around an invisible maypole to a menacing ritual.

'Three we'll close the shop,
Four we'll start to chop.
Ring around the green
Bring the one we've seen.'

At the end of each line each girl let go of her neighbour's hand and swiftly tapped herself on the right breast, the left breast, and between the legs. After the gesture had been repeated a dozen times it took on a sour air of religious parody.

The rhythm became an aggressive drum-tap. At the end of a verse there would be a stop, a lull, and a girl would drop out. Bronwen foresaw that the counting out and dissolving pattern would ultimately leave one girl isolated. When there were only three left, it became obvious which girl this would be. Something about the way two of the remaining dancers behaved, their cavorting and laughing, showed who was to be victim.

Her name was Carrie Lavater.

'Carrie . . . never going to marry?'

They danced, and she grinned fearfully back, and the trio became a whirling frenzy.

'Carrie . . . bring him home from sea?'

The older spectators had fallen silent. A gloating fear began to curdle in Bronwen's apprehension. She felt herself being ensnared in the communal trance.

Carrie Lavater cowered to the ground, while the other two leapt about her.

'Bring him back,' they exhorted her.

'No. No, I won't.'

'Home from the sea — Carrie'll dare to marry.'

Carrie put her hands over her ears. The girls who had dropped out of the dance reformed the circle and began to spin about her, arms at first at full stretch and then shortening until they crowded in upon her. One girl had picked up a stone, and again hands were swiftly released, the stone flicking from one cupped hand to another, going on its way as hands gripped and interwove again. The girls' voices were gentle now, placid in ritual fulfilment.

'Yours is the choice. To come freely — '

'No!'

'Or be sought out!'

'No!'

Carrie had flung her arms wide in despair. As the dizzily revolving circle slowed, a hand came out, and the stone was placed in Carrie's outstretched palm.

'Now you will bring him.'

Bronwen heard a harsh laughter as if the earth itself were heaving with amusement. Everyone was singing or humming or chuckling. Everyone save herself, and the bowed Carrie Lavater, was inured to the idea of selecting a sacrifice, and eager for the selection.

And Alexander Caspian: where did he stand? She reached out for him; thought she heard him; and then was buffeted by discord and delirium.

'No,' cried Carrie, 'no, I'll not.' Clutching the stone, she pushed away the two nearest girls and broke out of the ring. 'I'll not be the one.'

The faces of the girls, her friends, stared blank disbelief.

'I'll not do it, I'll not be chosen, I won't bring him.'

Torn away from the mesmerized circle, Carrie came face to face with Bronwen. Her free hand rose in a sign against the evil eye. The other thrust forward the stone.

'Let *her* be it. I put it upon her. You hear, all of you? All of you, you're witness, I'm laying it on *her*.' Three times the fingers jabbed. 'On her.'

Bronwen tried to free herself from the group pressing in about her. Nobody actually seized her or forced her in any particular direction, but they were hemming her in while Carrie willed her to take the stone . . . while each and every one of them willed her to take it.

Suddenly there was an opening. Caspian strode towards her and crooked his arm so that her arm could slide through it.

'Miss Powys.'

This time the path that was made for them was friendly. Everyone grinned. Everything had changed. The strangers were accepted now. Accepted as what? Bronwen saw the smirks and wide, wet eyes; and heard the uncontrollable inner glee.

A man patted Caspian's shoulder. 'Poppyhead tea, sir? Have a cup, it's good against the night air.'

A face bobbed in front of Bronwen. 'And you, miss? It's getting late, you need something warming, something against the ague.'

Caspian and Bronwen marched on towards the inn through their guard of honour. Yet she had agreed to nothing. The stone remained with Carrie. And what, after all, was the significance of a stone?

She felt them unwinding; felt the expulsion of breath, the slow ebb tide of exhaustion.

Fortrey and one of his assistants were rolling an empty barrel towards the cellar flap. Leah carried some pots indoors, and came out again as Caspian and Bronwen reached the entrance. She dodged to one side with a half scared, half derisive glance.

When that night comes . . .

Then this, thought Bronwen dazedly, had not been the night? This was only a forerunner, an advent ceremony in anticipation of some other shoddy festival in some perverse local calendar. She was so tired. It had been an untidy, irrational, and briefly frightening evening, which had ended in anticlimax. After her earlier presentiments she supposed she should feel relieved instead of being so unsettled and unsatisfied.

Of one thing she could be sure: whatever the sequel, she would not be here to see it.

6

The church bells were ringing for morning service. Bronwen had no intention of risking further humiliation. As she crossed the hall, Fortrey emerged yawning from his back room, and she set herself in his path.

'I'm expecting to leave by the mid-morning train tomorrow. Perhaps you'll have my bill ready for me at breakfast time.'

He rubbed a bleary eye, then shook his head. 'Didn't reckon you'd be going yet awhile, miss.'

Her arrival had been greeted with suspicion, she had been granted accommodation only because of Alexander Caspian's haughty overruling of all protest. Now the landlord sounded regretful about her plans for departure. It was as capricious as everything else about this inbred, unfathomable place.

'I'm afraid I must.'

'Not yet, miss.' His manner was one of stolid disbelief. 'Not yet you mustn't.' He went on into the bar, the matter closed so far as he was concerned. She heard him pushing benches about and then there was the clump of the counter flap slamming up against the wall.

Dr. Caspian appeared at the foot of the stairs, his coming as silent as the settling of a dark, richly marked moth on the banister rail.

'The smell of smoke and stewed eel has permeated every crevice in this establishment. Would you care to search for fresh air in my company, Miss Powys?'

They went out of The Griffin into the square, keeping their distance from old women and sleepy families straggling towards the church. In silence the two of them walked out of the village and on to the droveway.

The footprints had advanced still further during the night.

'At this rate,' said Bronwen, 'how long do you think it will take them to reach the market square — if that is their destination?'

Caspian took out his notebook and opened it at a double page covered with sketches and jottings.

'Yesterday I made a survey of the country on each side of Hexney. And I made some provocative discoveries.' He turned the page towards her so that she could see the diminutive but finely detailed map he had drawn. 'This droveway' — his left forefinger identified the line — 'cuts directly under the village, as we know. To the west it is intersected by the Peddar's Way, an old pre-Roman track.'

Bronwen tried to envisage the completion of the spiky geometrical shape. Something was missing, and she felt she ought to be able to guess what it was.

'Hexney,' he was saying, 'grew up near an intersection of trade routes.'

'Why not on them — at the crossroads, I mean?'

'That's what I asked myself.' He indicated that she should accompany him a little way up the slope until they stood by one of the ragged slits made in the wall by crumbling masonry. Through this was a view of the tip of the church tower.

'Now,' said Caspian, 'stand with your back to that and look between those trees, out across the fen. I did it from outside, from several miles out. That gave a clearer view, but you can verify the findings from here.' He pointed. 'What is that, exactly centred between those two mounds, and directly in line with the church tower behind you?'

Bronwen remembered the day she had gone to take pictures of Ramsey Abbey. 'They call it Hereward's Beacon, or something like that.'

'It dates from long before Hereward. An old pagan mound, I'd say. It's surprising that nobody built a monastery on it: they tended to set up their monastic houses on the old gods' properties. But at least we can say that Hexney church was fitted into the pattern.'

'Pattern?'

He showed her the page again. 'The church, the gap between those two mounds, the higher mound, all line up directly on the market cross in Withersey — which some still call the Devil's Thumb.'

'What significance does all this have?'

He propped the notebook on a jutting stone and sketched in another line; then another, close to where the railway line ran.

Bronwen stared. 'Isn't that the bit they call — '

'Peddar's Lode. Yes.'

'Where little Tommy — '

'Yes.' His pencil moved again. 'Project it this way as well, and what do we get?'

Two lines came to a point. Another crossed to make another neat point. The star pattern was familiar, lacking only a final crosspiece to close one side.

Bronwen said: 'When that line is complete, it'll make a pentacle.'

'And the line that is needed to finish it — to seal it?'

She glanced over her shoulder, moved her feet a few steps; and saw what he meant. 'The footprints! If they do turn in towards the market place, on a very slight arc . . . '

'Not enough of a curve to throw out the basic design.'

'If they do reach the square, the pentacle will be sealed.'

'Quite so.'

She sat down on a tussock of dry grass, while Caspian strode to the fringe of trees and bushes and gazed, the set of his shoulders defiant, across the fen. He appeared to be demanding some admission — or submission. What he had uncovered reminded her of some of her own experiences, some of the oddities she had observed and recorded during her travels: standing stones, hilltop towers, cairns, ruins, and abandoned chapels. Often she had detected what might have been a mystical web, the fabric of some prehistoric intuition more sophisticated than the sceptical nineteenth century could credit. Solid testimony in earth and stone to an invisible composition. It was a matter one feared to pursue: conceiving a universe one and indivisible, in which nothing happened by chance or by human will, where every stone had been set for a purpose and every tumulus or cathedral was an indispensable peg in a complex framework, was one presaging eternal serenity or eternal imprisonment for mankind?

Caspian turned and took up her thoughts. 'There are other places and other groupings which appear, on analysis, to have been . . . let us say designed. Even the most primitive human beings loved to play complicated games with their environment, setting problems for themselves and their successors.'

'Stonehenge?'

'Stonehenge for one,' he agreed. 'A mathematical puzzle in itself; and possibly an astronomical one also. But it is part of a still larger structure, aligned not merely on the axis of its own cult centre but absolutely straight on Avebury and a row of camps and tumuli right across country. Then there's Glastonbury: it is possible to trace a clumsy zodiac there, incorporating the abbey, the altar of the old abbey church, the tor, most of the main configurations of the town, and even South Cadbury. It might well appear less clumsy if certain features which have vanished over the centuries could be rediscovered and set in their original context.'

'And if every lost feature were restored,

you would still expect to find nothing but a man-made design?'

'What else should there be? Men playing throughout time with their fantasies.'

'Hexney,' said Bronwen: 'the things which have happened here, even in the few days you have been here, the whole feeling of the place . . . ?'

'One must not draw unscientific conclusions from inadequate evidence.'

'The footsteps,' she insisted. 'And that ceremony last night beginning something which didn't finish. Where does it all fit into your tidy sum?'

'There are factors missing, undeniably. That's the trouble with history. You use the evidence which has survived, and — '

'And force it to conform to your own prejudices.'

'Try by reasonable extension of known factors to fill in the gaps,' he corrected. She had the feeling that his argument was directed at himself rather than her. 'Hexney's position in the pentagram makes the sum a fairly commonplace one. Or let's see it rather as a relic of ancient geometry than a sum — sight lines and geographical features adopted by prehistoric track makers and adapted by successive generations. Long after their original purpose as landmarks and primitive religious boundaries has been forgotten, such sequences of dolmens and beacon and old burial clumps are bound to accumulate a great residue of superstition. But it's men who make the superstition, not superstition the men. It's all of it explicable in purely human terms.'

'All explicable?' Quietly she said: 'Why are you so intent on dismissing — '

'I dismiss nothing. I'm simply trying to correlate so-called mysteries and magic on a basis of science and mathematics.'

'It never occurs to you that the mathematics might *be* the magic?'

He smiled. Scrambling up and tugging her skirt straight, Bronwen heard herself snap the challenge: 'And into what pattern did the Devil's Footsteps fit in Devon?'

She was lashed by a sudden great, terrifying darkness rolling in from the back of his mind. Smitten and thrown up by it, she was poised for a moment above a fathomless whirlpool. Then he had drawn it back, fought it into submission, and thrown her aside.

'What was that?' she demanded, breathless. 'What *was* it?'

'What was what, Miss Powys?' His voice was too level, too painfully disciplined.

'What are you hiding? You're denying something — something that makes nonsense of all you've been saying. I've caught a whisper of it before. It keeps telling you more than you wish to hear.'

'The language of palmists and sooth-sayers doesn't suit you.'

He swung away and crouched again over the footprints his eyes following the line that they would have to take if they were indeed to complete the pentacle.

'Early November,' said Bronwen. 'Quite possibly the fifth of November. Guy Fawkes' Night.'

'So you've worked it out, too? A shrewd calculation. I congratulate you.'

'Not a calculation. I heard it from you.'

'Oh, dear. Oh, my dear Miss Powys, I

do wish you wouldn't — '

'I heard it from you. Direct from your own mind. Explain that, Dr. Caspian.'

He stood up. 'Obviously I must accept your word. I can only conclude that you are in closer sympathy with my researches than you pretend. People immersed in the same problem, with the same terms of reference, often arrive jointly at the same conclusion. In the most mundane affairs, members of the same family anticipate each other's remarks. And in more complicated matters, people who are close to each other — '

'Are we close?' The question fell from her lips before she had had time to decide whether it ought to be spoken.

It brought him to a stop. His self-confidence, always too strident, was shaken by doubt.

'I don't know. Miss Powys, I . . . I can't be sure. Can you?'

She was too frightened to answer: frightened not of him but of something within herself.

* * *

'Yes,' said the rector. 'Er, yes, we do have a rather . . . hm . . . unique festival on the fifth of November.'

The congregation this morning had clearly been small. Many of the villagers were sleeping off the effects of the night before. Mrs. Morritt and other tight-lipped stalwarts had come out scowling with self-righteousness, but ceased scowling as they passed Bronwen and Caspian. There were some sidelong, gloating smirks; and a few frank smiles — quite different from the carapace of hostility displayed until yesterday.

'A bonfire?' Caspian pressed Mr. Wint. 'A guy, and a fire, and that sort of thing?'

'That sort of thing, indeed. But some different elements, stemming from Hexney's own experiences.'

The rector was far from keen to talk about this local bonfire night. Perhaps, thought Bronwen, he had High Church leanings and disapproved of what were in essence anti-Papal demonstrations. But Alexander Caspian was patient and compelling. The three of them paced slowly down the path, and bit by bit the

140

story was extracted.

During the Great Plague that reached the fenlands in 1666, Hexney had been infected by a visitor from outside. As well as transmitting the poison of the pest, this unfortunate had evidently been responsible for the infectious mistrust of 'outsiders', which continued to run in the blood of the survivors' descendants. When the plague struck, it was given added strength by the malarial conditions of the surrounding fens. There were few contacts in those days with other hamlets, of which there were in any case very few, but Hexney itself was devastated. Only a handful of local families came through unscathed. Many victims were thrown into the fen, until it was pointed out that this might pollute the main source of Hexney's livelihood. Then some plague pits were dug near the priory ruins; and towards the end, when help and advice at last reached Hexney from outside, many bodies were burnt. Even now there was further suffering in store. A fumigatory fire, which had been enjoined on the village, in which clothes and household objects were to be destroyed, got out of hand. Hexney's plague, like London's, was followed by a conflagration in which a large part of the village was gutted and a number of living people were burnt to death. The tiny group of survivors slowly rebuilt the village, and eventually other people came to settle: but after many generations these would still be foreigners.

Memories of the disaster lingered, and over the years blended symbolically with the Guy Fawkes bonfire ritual. The rector fretfully admitted that the whole thing was basically pagan, like many of its kind. Shetland fires in January, the pagan bonfires of the winter solstice, the Beltane fire of returning summer — how little they differed from the debauchery at Lewes in Sussex, where the symbolic burning of the Pope was followed by the hurling of a blazing tar barrel into the river.

'A useful accommodation with the Celtic Samhain,' Caspian observed, 'when fire was doused by water to signify the conquest of summer by winter.'

The rector perked up slightly. The discussion became more abstract. Mr. Wint, like Dr. Caspian, appeared happiest when dealing in generalizations and academic theories from which the flesh and violence of reality had been purged. They commented on the sensible concentration of innumerable saints' days into one All Hallows Day, and found parallels with the concentration of pagan fire rituals into Guy Fawkes' Night. So tidy, thought Bronwen: so cosy and reasonable and all-explanatory . . . provided you turned a resolutely deaf ear to the undying undertones.

When they left the rector, with mutual expressions of goodwill, Bronwen said without preamble:

'And if men have created all these things, and then later made categories for them, and tidied up loose ends, don't you think there is a danger that they may have created something beyond themselves?'

'I fear you have lost me, Miss Powys.'

'You have never considered the possibility that the superstitions of which you spoke earlier, the patterns all made by men, could become something . . . something greater than the sum of its parts? Something good or' — she gestured towards the village wall, the pillory, the inn — 'wicked?'

Caspian shook his head.

'Even if a number of old villages, or old beacon sites, or all of them in conjunction, started out as you say, couldn't they become something *else*? The accretions of time, working on them . . . can't you believe there are some places, some whole regions, with too much history?' Again she was assaulted by a confusion of pictures, seen and photographed — individual architectural features and whole communities, shot through with something more real and more lasting than the buildings or their occupants. Each place had its own characteristic, fashioned from a living force that was more than stones and wood and flesh and mind. 'Thousands of private histories accumulating into something new,' she mused aloud. 'Memories left like permanent echoes on the air, and shaking that air, and shaking the very fabric just as Joshua shook the walls of Jericho. Why not? In a village like this set at the hub of this ancient pattern you've discovered, couldn't there be something beyond our ordinary calculations — with rituals and festivals not shown on the rector's calendar?'

He was watching her mouth with affectionate amusement. The affection was more galling than the amusement.

'Haunted!' She cried the word that had been secretly tormenting her ever since Tommy Dunstall's death. 'Why shouldn't we say it's haunted? The stones continue to resonate, sometimes the resonance of the past builds up until it cancels out the present. When the vibrations reach a certain pitch — '

'Vibrations!' His ready scorn was rekindled. 'A notion much favoured by spiritualists and other such charlatans.'

'Must they all be charlatans?'

'I have encountered no other.'

'You wouldn't accept that some mediums might be sincere, might sense things you don't?'

'I would not.'

'That they might be affected by some

force they genuinely cannot explain, and cannot control?'

'They use tricks,' he said flatly, 'for gain.'

'And there's nothing supernatural which will not sooner or later be explained by science? Nothing,' she said, 'in Hexney to be frightened of?'

'Nothing.'

★   ★   ★

She dreamed. Caspian was on his way to study the footprints again, determined this time to catch the hoaxer. She was swaying after him, calling to him to wait. It was night yet every rut and every twig was clearly discernible. When they reached the droveway it was also clear that the footmarks were advancing — coming on before their eyes, as deep now as chasms. She implored him to come away while there was still time; and he obeyed so quickly that they were snatched back, as if on a piece of elastic, to her room.

Now she was struggling against him, outraged by what she read in his mind yet wanting to laugh with him and knowing he could read her mind also and knew everything she thought about him. No, she protested. I am going away, she told him. He weighed down upon her. I am going back to Wales in the morning, she said. The weight increased. Not just Caspian but a score of others were holding her down. Why was she so sure that other people in the village were dreaming, and all dreaming of her and of a night yet to come? And now Carrie Lavater was at her bedside with one hand holding the sheet so that it was impossible to get out. Bronwen fought; and woke up with the blankets heavy on her, and the pillow damp with perspiration.

The inn was silent. She half expected a cry of help from Caspian, snared again in that deathly chill. But all was tranquil. Only the faintest rim of light showed between the curtains. She turned over and groped for the box of vestas by the candlestick. Her travelling-clock showed only two o'clock in the morning.

Reluctant to slip back into that same dream, she lit the candle. She would stay awake for a few minutes and think herself into a different frame of mind.

Her luggage was fastened up ready for departure in the morning. One case remained open for last-minute additions. On top lay the two books she had brought with her — Mr. George Meredith's extraordinary new novel, which required greater concentration than she had been able to muster during her stay here, and a thin volume of Lamb's essays which her father had given to her one Christmas. She got out of bed and picked up the volume of essays. Propped on one elbow with the pillow plumped up against her shoulder, she let the pages fall open at random.

'Gorgons, and Hydras, and Chimaeras . . .'

'Oh, goodness, no,' she murmured. But the paragraph lured her on.

' . . . dire stories of Celaeno and the Harpies, may reproduce themselves in the brain of superstition — but they were there before. They are transcripts, types — the archetypes are in us, and eternal. How else should the recital of that which we know in a waking sense to be fake come to affect us at all? Is it that we naturally conceive terror from such objects, considered in their capacity of being able to inflict upon us bodily injury? O, least of all! These terrors are of older standing. They date beyond body — or without the body, they would have been the same.'

Bronwen snapped the book shut. She could not bring herself to slide out of bed again, but put the book on the bedside chest and blew out the candle.

She lay awake for a time she could not estimate in the darkness, trying to force herself to think of the journey home, the unpacking, the everyday chores she would have to tackle. In sleep something would be waiting for her. They were there before . . . they date beyond body . . . She made herself see the towers of Caernarvon castle, and the butcher's shop below the walls, and Jones the greengrocer.

She slept.

When she awoke, it was broad daylight. She looked at her clock.

It could not be that late; could not possibly be so.

Downstairs there was the shuffle of feet. A door slammed, there was a clank of bottles. Outside, the milk cart rattled across the square. Somebody shouted something, somebody laughed.

She had overslept. She had missed her train — had been made to miss her train.

7

'Why was I not woken?'

'You didn't say nothing about wanting a call, miss.'

'You knew I intended to leave. When I was late coming down you must surely have realized — '

'Took it you'd had your mind changed, miss.'

There was no way of penetrating Fortrey's odious self-righteousness. But she would not give him the satisfaction of seeing her collapse into feminine flutters. Curtly she said:

'There's another train this morning?'

'Not till the afternoon, miss. Don't know as it would get you anywhere special.'

'I shall take it.'

He shrugged, confident that she would not, and went on his way out to the stable yard.

Caspian passed him in the entrance.

'Good morning, Miss Powys. I quite thought you'd be on your way by this time.'

It was too much to bear. She had kept her self-control before the landlord, but this extra jibe maddened her. 'You knew I would still be here,' she blazed. 'You very well knew I would not be on my way.'

He was taken aback. 'On the contrary. As I recall, we made our farewells last evening — '

'And then what? You're one of them. You . . . the shame of it! You were one of them, preventing my leaving.'

'Miss Powys, I do assure you I have been out since early this morning, continuing my investigations.'

'And before that? During the dark hours, holding me captive — mentally imprisoning me so that . . . In dreams,' she cried. 'Could anything be more cowardly?'

His expression of shock was coloured by a darker perturbation, a current beating up from the sombre pools of his eyes.

'You had a dream last night?'

152

'You know I did.'

'I know that I did. But I had not thought . . . ' He checked himself, and it was the first time he had refused to meet her gaze with the arrogant mockery of his own. 'It could hardly have been the same.'

'Could it not?'

'A man needs great self-discipline in your presence, Miss Powys. Waking, he must exercise that self-discipline. But he is not to be blamed for the waywardness of his dreams.'

'I am leaving,' she said. 'Whatever may have been done to make me miss this morning's train, I shall not fail to be on this afternoon's.'

A twist of humour touched his lips again. 'I strongly advise against it.'

'Advice now, rather than force?'

'I would not dream' — the word was accompanied by a wry grimace — 'of forcing you to miss yet another train. But the one this afternoon happens to go in the opposite direction from that which I fancy you require.'

Words failed her. She stormed out into the open, looking round the marketplace and hating every stick and stone of it.

There was nobody about. The Gathering over and Sunday over, the men were all back at work. It was a normal, depressed, depressing, backward little village: frightening only in its drab ordinariness.

She would hire a trap to take her to Withersey. From the junction there must be a way of getting at least to Shrewsbury, where she could stay overnight with a cousin and then proceed into Wales the following day.

But the carter was out, and his wife did not know when he would be back.

The joiner's handcart would suffice for conveying her luggage and equipment to the railway halt. Even if she had to set off in entirely the wrong direction, she would leave Hexney today. There must be a roundabout route that would eventually lead her towards home. And if she had to stay in some Norfolk seaside resort for the night, it would be better — anything would be better — than remaining in Hexney, a prey to the laziness and gloating derision of the villagers.

First she must find, at the halt, just where the afternoon train would take her. Doubtless Fortrey would know; but doubtless he would take pleasure in misleading her.

Bronwen crossed the square to the gateway and stepped under the arch.

It was as if a pall of numbing mist had fallen upon her shoulders and then slid down to envelop her completely. She struggled for breath, and the chill of it stung her throat. She made herself take another step forward. Her toes scraped only a couple of inches over the cobbles.

Below, the hill fell away between two rows of squat little houses, built outside the village wall in this century. Bronwen could have sworn that all the doors and windows were tightly shut when she reached the gateway. Now several were open: a door on this side, two lower windows on that, an upper window some three or four houses down the terrace. A stooped old woman stood on one doorstep. Two younger women leaned on windowsills above the road, leaning out, waiting.

If she did succeed in thrusting her way through this frozen portcullis, there would be a gauntlet to run.

They would not dare to touch her.

Or was it that they would not dare to let her pass?

She had the right to leave this village. There was no power on earth to stop her. Here was the exit from the village, there was the slope and down there, at the end of the meandering causeway, was the tiny station from which she could leave when she chose — or when a train from the outside world chose to arrive and depart. She would now prove that she could walk down the hill and make her own arrangements and return and leave again, this time finally.

Her right leg tensed but would not move. As in the dream last night, her limbs were trapped. The freezing mist congealed. Soon she would be able to go neither forwards nor backwards.

I will get there, she urged herself: I will put one foot in front of the other, I will walk down that hill and I will reach the station and I will wait there, and if necessary I will leave without one case, one scrap of my belongings, and when I am safe I will send for them to be forwarded to me. It's easy. All I have to do is walk.

And spend an hour, two or three hours, on Hexney Halt. With Mrs. Dunstall in her cottage; Mrs. Dunstall coming out of her cottage, Mrs. Dunstall pouring out her superstitious hatred.

I will tell her all the calm, scientific things Dr. Alexander Caspian has told me.

There was a rumble of wheels and the clatter of empty milk churns behind her. She had been unable to move, but now she was released. She edged sideways, and the milk cart rumbled through the gateway.

She shouted. He could take her down, she would make her peace with Mrs. Dunstall, they would dismiss the horrors . . .

The milkman paid no attention. He had broken through the barrier without effort, and was gone. The women on the doorsteps and in the windows did not so much as turn their heads to watch him on his way. They stood and leaned, leisurely and contemplative, with their eyes idly fixed on a patch of road that Bronwen would have to traverse if she wished to attain Hexney Halt.

She dragged herself back. The mist that had clogged her limbs when she wished to move on down the slope now dissolved and gracefully relinquished her. There was nothing to stop her making her peace with Hexney: nothing to choke the way into Hexney as it choked the way out.

In daylight, her cheeks feeling the bite of the fitful wind and her shoes prodded and misdirected by the hard, uneven cobbles, she could not still be dreaming.

She walked back the way she had come but refused to go back into The Griffin. Not yet. Not to give Fortrey the satisfaction of an 'I told you so'. Instead she went on, past the church and down the lane, until she stood above the priory ruins. If the worst came to the worst she could walk over the grass, down that slope, and go right round the village.

And face the footsteps coming the other way, coming relentlessly towards her?

The innocent grass took on a lustre of sour green treachery. As well walk on that as on a quagmire.

I must go. She reiterated it to herself. I have nothing to fear, nothing but my own misapprehensions. I . . . refuse . . . to remain . . . in Hexney.

Do you hear me?

She went back to The Griffin.

Caspian was seated in the nook beside the main fireplace counting out coins on to a saucer. He raised his head, smiled, and stood up.

'Miss Powys, I believe I can offer some small assistance.'

'You can release me. You and the others.'

She sensed his inner disturbance and his rejection of all that she accused him of. 'Please calm yourself. I am part of no conspiracy. Nor do I credit the existence of any such conspiracy.'

'I intend to leave.'

'Just so. And I have to acquaint you with one weekly event, which our host has hitherto omitted to mention. It is Monday; and at thirty minutes past noon on a Monday the Cambridge diligence

159

passes through Hexney.'

She could not at first take it in. Confusedly she said: 'I shall not be allowed on it.'

'Miss Powys, I have taken the liberty of instructing Mr. Fortrey not to let it depart until you have taken your seat.'

'You . . . they . . . I can't get *out*. Don't pretend you don't know. If I try to go through the gateway, I am stopped. If I were to risk setting foot on the ground outside the village, I . . . ' Tears choked in her throat.

He took her arm and guided her towards a chair by the window. She sat, shaking uncontrollably, until he had hurried away and returned with a glass of brandy. As the spirit burned its way through the congestion, he said, very slowly and deliberately:

'Miss Powys, you said you were disturbed last night by dreams.'

She nodded, not trusting herself to speak.

'And you felt that you were being prevented from leaving this place?'

'You know that.' Her voice was harsh and splintered.

He did not argue but went levelly on: 'Apart from your nightmares, did you have a sound night's sleep?' When she did not answer, he insisted: 'Miss Powys, did you wake up at all?'

Again she nodded.

'And stayed awake for a time? For a long time, perhaps?'

'I . . .'

'For long enough to tire yourself, to lose count of time — to oversleep in compensation?'

'I merely read a few short passages, and went to sleep in a very short time.'

'You read something soothing?'

'A portion of one of Lamb's essays.'

'Innocuous, one would suppose. Which essay?' When again she did not reply, he pressed her again: 'Which essay was it, dear lady?'

She whispered it. ' "Witches and Other Night-Fears".'

He put his head back and laughed outrageously. 'Oh, my dear Miss Powys! Do I really need to explain your nightmares and your exhaustion this morning?'

She would gladly have thrown the glass

at him; but she had drunk the brandy he provided, and it warmed her, and if she felt well enough to be angry then it was largely due to his kindness. Yet she could not bear to be treated as an impressionable child when she knew . . .

What did she know?

He was saying: 'You will have a companion to see you safely out of the village. I have decided to leave also. I shall spend a day in Cambridge with an old friend, checking one or two historical aspects of this peculiar place, before I return to London. Either you can come to Cambridge and seek transport from there on, or you can be put down at Withersey.'

'From Withersey,' she said, 'I can surely get to Shrewsbury.'

'Then your mind is now at rest?'

'It seems,' said Bronwen with an effort, 'that I am once again indebted to you for arranging my transport.'

She was glad to escape upstairs, on the excuse of finishing her packing. The window was open, and the morning smelt fresh and invigorating. The phantasms of the night had evaporated. Across the square the gateway was bathed in limpid sunshine.

Ashamed of her own panic she turned to the wardrobe to take out her dressing gown and lay it on the clothes already folded in the open case.

There was a crash and tinkling of broken glass. A handful of stones showered in through the open section of the window; others smashed through the remaining panes, falling, skidding across the carpet.

Bronwen let the dressing gown crumple through her fingers. Then she hurried to the window.

There was the flutter of a blue skirt on the corner of the lane, a few yards to her left; then it was gone.

Footsteps tapped along the passage. Knuckles rapped on her door, and Mrs. Fortrey said: 'Are you all right, miss? You had an accident?'

When Bronwen did not answer, the door opened. Mrs. Fortrey stared at the shards of glass, and the jagged holes in the window.

'Well, whatever . . . ?'

'Somebody threw stones in at me.'

'But who'd want to do that?' Mrs. Fortrey came closer to examine the mess. 'Well, I never. I thought you'd dropped some of them bits and pieces of yours. Whoever, now . . . ?' There was a note of accusation in her voice as, grumbling, she went down on her knees and began to pick up the small pebbles and a few sharp flints.

Bronwen pushed the last few items into her case and slammed the lid down.

'And poltergeists now?' said Alexander Caspian as she began to tell him the story while they waited for the coach to set off from The Griffin.

His barely repressed amusement brought her to a stop. She sat upright, determined to exchange no further words with him. They would stop at Withersey and she would get down, and they would say goodbye — again, and this time definitively.

It felt strange. Somehow they had drawn too close in this short time: too close for conventional handshakes, for the formal goodbye and the insincere promise that they would meet again one day.

The horses' hoofs scrabbled on the

smooth cobbles, gripped, and the coach lumbered forward. Bronwen did not dare to look out of the window. She knew when the vehicle would turn, when horses and wheels would swing towards the gateway and slow, easing through so that neither side should scrape the ragged stonework.

Outside the women would be waiting.

She held her breath, aware that Caspian was glancing at her. She refused to return the glance.

Shadows of the gateway darkened over the coach. The wheels were scarcely turning. They were going to come to a halt. At any moment the chill would flood into the coach.

Then they tilted forward, began to increase speed; and there was the squeak of the brake being applied to hold them steady down the hill.

'You see,' said Caspian quietly: 'we are free.'

Two old men and a starchy middle-aged woman sitting opposite stared at them.

Keeping her voice even lower, Bronwen said: 'Thank you.'

'It was all in your imaginings.'

'No. We are out only because there were two of us. Because the place is . . . not ready yet. Not strong enough, yet, to resist two of us.'

'The two of us.' He leaned closer, humouring her. 'Yes, we would make an impressive partnership, would we not?'

She would have drawn sharply away, but did not wish to create any impression, unfavourable or otherwise, on the three other passengers.

'I was speaking.' said Caspian, 'of a professional partnership.'

'Sir?'

He was taking a card from his wallet, 'If ever you should come to London, Miss Powys, I do beg you to do me the honour of calling upon me.' He handed her the card.

She would have liked to appear haughty and indifferent after all that had occurred. But curiosity was — after all that had occurred — too much for her. She looked down at the florid lettering.

COUNT CASPAR
Master of Prestidigitation
and Illusion

The Cavern of Mystery
Leicester Square
London

She looked up.

'I did tell you that I was a magician,' he reminded her.

⋆   ⋆   ⋆

Joshua Serpell had squeezed himself back against the outer arch to watch them go. As Mrs. Morritt crossed the square with her shopping basket he looked in at her.

'I reckon we'll see them back. She'll be brought back here sure enough, when it's nigh on time.'

Then he wiped a hand across his eyes and shuffled in through the gateway, wondering whatever had made him say a thing like that.

PART II

The Droveways

1

Outside the theatre a huge poster dominated the façade and was itself dominated by the huge representation of a bearded man with burning eyes, his arms spread to raise a scarlet-lined cloak above a wild fandango of Oriental slaves, dancing maidens, a decapitated prince, flying birdcages, a trunk with swords plunged through it, and other figures and objects larger than life. The greenish glow of gas-lamps about Leicester Square paled under the harshness of a hundred incandescent bulbs blazing upon the bacchanal of the poster and its lettering, which against a fiery background proclaimed:

THE CAVERN OF MYSTERY
presents
each Monday and all the week
the original
unsurpassed
incomparable

171

COUNT CASPAR
in his celebrated panorama of
prestidigitation and his challenge
to all self-proclaimed soothsayers,
mediums, levitationists and apporteurs
to surpass him in wizardry.
Doors open at 7.30. Commence at 7.45.
Carriages at 10.30

Inside, a young man in baggy panta-
loons and a pink-cheeked Columbine danced
across the stage, never still, circling a large
round table from which they plucked one
item after another. The man twirled a
newspaper into a cone between skilful fingers, tilted it towards the audience to show
that it was empty, and beckoned the girl
on. She pirouetted before him, then reached
for the cone and began to draw flowers
and fruit from the depths of an apparently
bottomless cornucopia.

Before the applause had died away,
music from the orchestra pit sparkled up
into a waltz and the young buffoon began
to pour wine from a full glass back into
an empty bottle on the table, while
Columbine fashioned two paper cylinders

and fastened them with pins. Lightly she dropped one over the glass, one over the bottle. The music stopped. Her partner waved one hand above the hidden bottle, the other above the cylinder concealing the glass. There was a loud, long-held chord from the orchestra. The girl darted forward and lifted the cylinder from the glass — to reveal the bottle. She made a moue at the audience as the man lifted the other paper shield to reveal the glass, still with its half measure of wine undisturbed in spite of its swift transposition. The orchestra played the opening bars of a gallop while the papers were again dropped over glass and bottle; which again exchanged places. As applause rolled up from the auditorium the girl threw both cylinders in the air and, as they fell, caught them and tore them up.

Stagehands ran on to clear away material, and moved the table itself a few feet closer to the wings. The young man, bouncing back alone for a farewell spattering of applause, carried a large tablecloth over his left arm. He rubbed his right hand across the table to show that it was bare, then shook out the cloth and flourished it like a cape. When the folds dropped on to the table there was at first too much towards the front of the stage, trailing over the boards. He moved round, tugging and, adjusting, and at last pulled the cloth up until its hem was even all round. People in the stalls could now see his legs moving behind the table.

The orchestra stopped in the middle of a bar.

'You're all waiting for Count Caspar.'

There was a rumble of agreement, topped by a shout from the gallery: 'Aye, that we are.'

The young man paced about the stage, miming a search. Twice he returned to the table and lifted the edge of the cloth to demonstrate that there was nobody underneath. Then, apparently baffled, he walked off stage.

Lights turned crimson and there came a reflection of leaping flames on the back-cloth. Scurrying arpeggios on the flute reached piercing heights. Then, hunched in the fiery glow, the cloth began slowly to peak up from the centre of the table. The folds shaped themselves to a human head and shoulders, and went on rising. Suddenly hands emerged from beneath the hem to grip the cloth and hurl it aside.

Standing with arms outstretched, so that in the swirling light and shadow all that was visible was the red lining of his cloak, Count Caspar smiled acknowledgment of the welcoming shouts and a great organ chord from the orchestra.

Lights came fully on. He seemed not so much to leap as to float down from the table. Four stagehands in billycock hats marched on carrying a large trunk, making a great performance of setting it down behind Caspar. One of them, in a fit of apparent abstraction, took off his hat and laid it upside down on the table. Count Caspar picked it up, inspected the interior, and held it out so that the audience might see it was empty. He then began to produce rabbits from the interior, handing them out so fast to the nearest stagehand that the man could not cope but had hurriedly to pass each one to his neighbour. At the same time the men were manoeuvring the trunk into a fresh position. Two men came on to remove the table, and the act finished with the audience unsure whom to watch — the harassed stage hands, forming a sort of chain to dispose of rabbits, eggs and coloured streamers emerging from the hat, or the magician himself, dexterously maintaining a non-stop stream of discoveries.

At last the supply dried up. While the audience clapped, Caspar offered the hat back to the stagehand who had set it down. The man refused to accept it, peering suspiciously into the lining. As laughter welled up, the magician became enraged. He shouted at one of his other assistants who, after seeming to plead with him, went with bowed head into the wings and returned with a slim rapier. Caspar snatched the rapier and launched himself at the erring stagehand, who was clutching his hat to his stomach. The point of the sword touched the hat; the man appeared to grab the point in terror, but the supple blade, neatly guided into the tubing curved to fit his left hip, emerged from his back. He reeled off into the wings, and another stagehand with an impassive white face came on to take over his duties.

A clap of thunder from the flies and a sonorous drum roll from the orchestra drove the stagehands off, and Columbine returned to offer Count Caspar a pretty curtsy.

He advanced to the footlights.

'Before I dispose of this young lady, I would like to ask for the assistance of a committee. Four gentlemen, please, from the audience. I invite you to study every move we make here on stage, and tell your friends if you can explain how we achieve our ends.'

There was the usual moment of reluctance, of wives nudging husbands and men pretending they were not prepared to make fools of themselves; and then three men from the stalls edged out into the aisle, and someone from the back came hurrying down towards the stage.

'Please examine this trunk,' said Caspar. 'Take as much time as you require. I would like your confirmation that there is no concealed mechanism — that this is simply an ordinary trunk.'

The four prodded the trunk, rapped it with their knuckles, opened it and peered inside. They professed themselves satisfied. Caspar held the lid open and waved commandingly at Columbine. She stepped daintily over the edge and stood in the trunk. At another command she sat down, then stretched herself out as far as she could, her knees drawn up and feet braced against one end. The lid was lowered, and Caspar offered a key to one of the committee.

'I depute you to watch the lock, and be sure there is no time trigger to make it fly open when no one is looking.'

Two stagehands appeared and began to lash ropes about the trunk. As they tilted it up on one end and strained to tighten a knot, Caspar set about addressing the audience on his regrets at the loss of such a beautiful assistant, the need to advertise for a replacement . . . swaggering up and down, half distracting the supposedly watchful committee.

Where ropes crossed, wax seals were affixed. The tablecloth that had done service earlier was produced and fastened around the trunk with leather straps. The volunteers were invited to inspect the brass buckles closely, and finally the whole thing was lifted by the two panting stagehands and set down with a heavy thud across two trestles.

Caspar paced around it three times. Then he drew a thin willow wand from beneath his cloak. The orchestra slid through a minor cadence into silence.

Fireworks spouted brilliantly from the end of the wand, finishing with a crack that echoed through the theatre.

'She is gone,' cried Caspar. 'Farewell!'

He waved the committee towards the trunks and its wrappings; they fumbled their way through the leather straps but could not unfasten the knots. A stagehand returned to slacken the ropes. The key was turned in the lock, and the lid thrown back.

The trunk was empty.

The stagehand, needing no assistance with this demonstrably lighter weight, tipped it off the trestles and stood it on end again, open to the audience.

As applause rolled down the aisle, it

was accompanied by the figure of Columbine, entering from the back of die stalls and tripping gaily towards the stage, where both she and Caspar shook hands with the four members of the volunteer committee.

The tempo quickened. Two young jugglers entertained the audience while more cabinets were manhandled into position. Caspar escaped from ropes and manacles; a tumbler performed dizzying feats on a make-believe mantelpiece; and there was a five-minute polka from the dancing phantoms. The show concluded with a pageant of history: the escape of Robin Hood from chains in a dungeon, the release of two victims from a Spanish torture chamber, the levitation of King Arthur's Round Table, and the execution of Anne Boleyn — in which the severed head was held up for all to see, and then replaced on the body.

Count Caspar shook the cloak from his shoulders as he went down the three stone steps to the dressing room corridor. At the same time he shook the flamboyant personality of the magician aside, and became a tired, but ever critical, technician.

'My entrance was very nearly bungled.'

'I know, Doctor, I know. We were all very upset.'

'What the devil went wrong?'

'The pulley in the left front leg of the table jammed. Billy had to adjust die weights and jerk it free.'

'Only just in time. If the tablecloth had been levelled out two seconds earlier, they'd have seen me kneeling in the cradle on its way up.'

'I'll take it to pieces myself, Doctor. This very night.'

Louis Mordecai was as distressed as the magician. Senior craftsman of the Count Caspar organization, in charge of all the most delicate mechanisms in the theatre, he felt every snag as painfully as the performers on stage. His sallow face, dwindling away to a sharply pointed chin, was like that of an emaciated marmoset shrivelling to a more and more melancholy state at a harsh word from his master.

'And the trapdoor squeaked in the

trunk sequence. I had to chatter like a madman to cover it.'

'I didn't hear that. But it'll be seen to, Doctor, it'll be seen to.'

Caspian allowed himself a grin. 'I know it will, Louis. Well — what sort of house did we have tonight? Financially, I mean.'

'Takings a little down.'

'How much down?'

'Ten per cent on last week.'

'I don't call that a little.'

'It's the new show, Doctor. Mordecai's nose wrinkled nervously. 'Those American spiritualists at the Tabernacle.'

'Spiritualists!' It came out as a snarl.

'Doing very good business, I hear. I've heard it said, too, that it's because people like the idea of it being real and not just tricks — er, skill . . . '

'Real?'

'Well, you know what people will believe.'

'Yes, I do know what people will believe. And I think it's our duty to show them the folly of their beliefs. I think, Louis, one of us must go to the Tabernacle and make a note of all their specialities. And another of us should attend one of their private séances — where I understand the seats are far more expensive.'

'They do say you get value for money.'

'Do they?' said Dr. Alexander Caspian. 'Do they, indeed? Then let us see how we can match them.'

★ ★ ★

The Chesterfield twins had taken a suite of rooms in Russell Square, not too far from the Holborn Tabernacle in which their public meetings were regaled with table turning, spirit rappings and a variety of psychic messages. Fortunately it was not too far either, from Caspian's own theatre in Leicester Square. He would have ample time after the séance to get back and change for the evening performance.

A fine clinging mist seeped up the streets from the river thickening with a change of temperature and an early lighting of fires, and with cloudy yellow miasmas rising from the gutters and sewers of the city. Rather than use his own curricle, whose red and gilded ornamentation might betray his identity to the Chesterfields, Caspian took a hansom cab and arrived with five minutes to spare. He leaned on a stick and wobbled his head as he counted out the fare from a little leather purse. His hair was streaked with silver and a dirty grey; his beard was tangled. One of his legs dragged slightly as he went up the steps to the door.

Ahead of him, already tugging the bell pull, was a distraught-looking elderly man, as genuinely unkempt and shaky as Caspian's impersonation. When a maid opened the door he burst out at once:

'Is there to be a sitting this afternoon? It's so urgent, I must *try* to get through.'

'You've made an appointment, sir?'

'No, no, I haven't. But if you will tell them — tell Mr. Chesterfield and his sister, please — I need their help so much, I've heard such wonderful things about them . . . '

'You'll have to make an appointment,

sir. Mr. and Miss Chesterfield are very much in demand.' She looked past him. 'And you, sir?'

'Dr. Alexander,' wheezed Caspian. 'I think I am expected.'

'Come in, sir.'

The other man tried to pluck at her sleeve. 'But please, I do so want — '

'If you'll wait a minute, sir, I'll see if Mr. Leon can make a day for you.'

Caspian was shown into a small room with closed double doors occupying almost the whole of one wall. Against two of the other walls were set a number of satinwood chairs, on which four women and two men were waiting. They nodded shyly at the newcomer; and one middle-aged man went on talking in an undertone to the woman on his left, clearly his wife. The hushed atmosphere was that of a prayer meeting about to start.

The double doors opened just far enough to admit a thickset man with mutton-chop whiskers above a high starched collar, a diamond pin glinting in his silk cravat.

'Ah, well now. I guess that makes our little gathering complete. You'd be Dr. Alexander. I'm delighted to make your acquaintance. Delighted.'

'And I yours, sir.' Caspian coughed and wiped his eyes. 'It was good of you to accommodate me at only a few days' notice.'

'We try to provide balm for the bereaved,' said Leon Chesterfield. He pushed the doors wider. His own voice sank reverently. 'It was explained to you when you fixed to come and sit with us that, although it would offend the great spiritual principle for us to offer our psychic services for gain, we do accept contributions to cover the mundane expenses of this sadly materialistic world?'

There was a humble murmur of agreement.

Thus reassured, Mr. Chesterfield stood aside and let them file past him.

The windows of the room within had been masked by black hangings. The only light came from a purple-shaded gas jet, turned low, allowing just enough visibility for the visitors to find their way to the table in the centre. It was a circular mahogany table with a central leg and three clawed feet, with chairs set about it. Leon Chesterfield guided each of them to a place, leaving one for himself. Then, after a dramatic pause, he took a deep breath and went to a gap in the curtains through which he led his sister Letitia, clad in a billowing mauve dress which susurrated about her as she was led to an armchair set back from the others. Enough space under those shapeless folds, thought Caspian sourly, for a whole armoury of gadgets.

Leon dimmed the light almost to extinction, and picked his way carefully to the vacant seat. He had a woman on his right, Caspian on his left.

'Let us join hands and prepare.'

His left hand settled, cool and damp, above Caspian's.

The man on the far side of the table, in a diffident West Country accent, said: 'Do we have to go through this all in the dark? My lad was used to the light when he was alive, I don't see why — '

'The spirits do not speak readily in a

bright light,' said Leon. 'They are now accustomed to the shades.'

'But — '

'I have to put it to you straight,' said Letitia Chesterfield in a plaintive sigh. 'Maybe there aren't going to be any manifestations today. We get a sceptic, and we get a lot of disturbance to the odic waves.'

The man mumbled a repudiation of any idea that he might be a sceptic.

Leon gave them all the chance to settle and purge their minds of unworthy criticism. Then, taking his hand from Caspian's, he said: 'I have here a slate. Not a word on it. That slate's staying on my knees in case there's a spirit minded to write some message on it.'

'Maybe there'll be no manifestations today,' Miss Letitia warned for the second time.

There was a long pause. Caspian was so intent on picking up each slightest sound from the other sitters and from Letitia Chesterfield, sitting well back from them, that for a while he forgot to maintain his own stertorous breathing.

Abruptly he managed a rasp and a cough, and fidgeted on his chair.

As if to assuage his impatience there was a tinkling of bells near the ceiling. Instinctively everyone squinted up into the darkness. Leon intoned:

'Please be still. Let us be still and hearken.'

The room was in almost complete darkness save for a pinpoint of light in a crystal globe that had been set on a table before Letitia. Her eyes closed, she began to breathe heavily and rhythmically.

Caspian felt the faintest tensing in Leon's fingers. Leon's left boot was set against his own foot, and there too he felt a taut readiness.

Under their hands the round table moved. At first it was the gentlest of rocking motions. Then, without warning, it tilted to one side, quivered, and began to rock violently.

'Be still,' Leon urged in a whisper. 'And press down hard.'

The table thrust up, their hands slithered as they tried to steady it. Caspian felt Leon's hand snatched away;

then two fingers sought his again, and clamped down.

There was the squeak of chalk against the slate. It ceased, and then a tambourine jangled over their heads. One of the women let out a little squeak. Caspian felt something brush the hair at the back of his neck; the woman on his left jumped and he knew it must also have grazed her in passing.

Letitia Chesterfield said: 'Is there anybody there?'

Something too solid to be regarded as an ethereal finger jabbed Caspian's knee. Leon's big toe, he decided to his own satisfaction; though Leon's boot was still wedged against his. The light within the crystal ball intensified. Letitia's eyes, upturned and ecstatic, swam in the haze.

'Caroline?' she whispered. 'Did you say Caroline?'

The woman on Caspian's left let out a whimper. 'Caroline? Oh, please speak to me. Tell me, quickly, please . . . '

'Let us not harass the spirits,' said Leon.

Letitia's head bowed closer to the globe. 'Are you there, Caroline? Do you

190

have a message for a loved one?'

There was an odd scratching and crackling in mid-air, and out of nowhere came the sweet scent of honeysuckle. A moment later, something was tossed over Leon's shoulder on to the table.

'Caroline always loved honeysuckle,' breathed the woman.

'And still does.'

Shadows drifted across the surface of the ball, distorted by its curvature. But the unmistakable contours of a human face shaped themselves, brightening second by second, with the mouth pulled back in a long smile. Over the scent of honeysuckle came the cloying fumes of incense or joss sticks, and smoke drifted before Letitia's rapt face. Caspian turned his head to get a full view, in spite of a warning squeeze from Leon's fingers. He had to concede a reluctant admiration. They knew what they were about, these skilful twins.

The smoke not only provided an occult blur over the photograph now projected on to the crystal ball, but its reek disguised the hot metallic smell of the phantasmagoric lantern which must be concealed behind the black velvet hangings.

Gradually the picture faded. The woman was sobbing her gratitude.

'Is there any message for us?' ventured the husband of the married couple. 'If our boy's over there, if he's got anything he could confide in his mother and myself . . . '

'We cannot demand the blessing of communication,' Leon chided. 'We must be humble, and pray; and accept.'

The crystal was darkening. Letitia remained bowed in meditation over it. Then her head jerked back.

'There is somebody asking for . . . can it be 'Hussar'?' she asked in bright innocence.

Caspian said: 'I am 'Hussar'.'

He could just make out the shadowy blob of Leon's head turning a few degrees towards him. 'Dr. Alexander?'

'It was a pet name.'

'Letitia could not possibly have known that.' Leon drew obsequious attention to his sister's integrity.

'Somebody grieves for your grief,'

droned Letitia. 'She wants you to know that all is well. She is happy and fulfilled. Her spirit body has gathered itself in and is complete. No more duelling, she says. You know what that means?'

'Yes, I know what it means.'

'Little sister Rebecca was waiting to meet her. You know of Rebecca?'

'I do.'

'There will be more. She promises more, but she is still unused to the psychic enervation. She asks you to come again. And she says she is happy you kept your promise and are resisting no longer. You will know what that means, too?'

'Yes, I know what that means.' Caspian freed himself from the hands on either side and stood up. 'It means,' he said loudly, 'that the girl you sent round to my house in St. James's, pretending to have mixed up addresses and to be looking for another Dr. Alexander, earned her fee. She asked my housekeeper the most cunning questions. You were not to know that I had already supplied the housekeeper with a range of cunning answers. And the rest of these gullible sitters — '

'We have given these sad folk comfort,' rasped Leon in a tone very different from his suave incantatory one, 'and you defile their happiness.'

'Let's have the lights on,' said the man who had expressed mild protest at the start. 'I've been having a few doubts myself.'

Leon pushed himself away from the table and turned up the tap of the gas bracket. In the bright flare Letitia sat rocking to and fro, clutching her stomach. 'I knew our spirit guides were disturbed this evening. We could sense disbelievers present.'

In his left hand Leon held the slate, which he had tucked under the table at the beginning of the séance.

'Here!' He slammed it on the table before the married couple. 'That was coming through when our rapport was smashed by this blasphemer. What do you make of that?'

Caspian, reading words upside down from where he stood, made out a scrawled *Love . . . garden of joy . . . Stephen . . .*

The woman let out a sob. 'Stephen! It

was Stephen. Speaking to us — and the garden, he was going to tell us — '

'He was going to tell you' — Caspian cut her brutally short — 'a few things which in some way or other you had already let slip to the Chesterfield emissaries. Why do you suppose they accept sitters only at several days' notice? So that they can dig out facts on which to build their fantasies. And why — '

'Who are you?' asked Letitia faintly.

'I am Count Caspar, of the Cavern of Mystery.'

'A mocker.'

'Where mockery is merited, yes.'

'The spirits will deal with those who besmirch them.'

'I invite you all to my theatre one week from now.' Caspian spread his arms. 'And I invite any of you to join the committee which sits on stage and tries to unravel my magic. I challenge you to fault me in the reproduction of the illusions experienced in this room, or performed by these petty thaumaturges in their so-called Tabernacle. And I specifically challenge you, sir, and you, madam, here or anywhere else, to devise one feat which I cannot emulate to perfection within seven days — by the application of scientific principles and without mumbo-jumbo.'

He swept towards the door.

'The spirits,' Leon Chesterfield cried after him, 'will have the last word.'

★   ★   ★

'And they'll send their claque along here to shout you down and distract you, Doctor.'

It was Louis Mordecai, returned from a public display at the Tabernacle with news of a complicated table-rapping sequence and of supposedly ectoplasmic manifestations which he praised highly, not sure whether to imitate them with the use of cheese-cloth or by means of a variation on the 'Pepper's Ghost' illusion. He stood beside Caspian at the drawing board, watching a diagram positioning mirrors and sheets of plate glass take shape.

'Let them hire every claqueur from every street in London,' said Caspian.

'And let them beware. How do they know I'll not produce a man-eating tiger from my opera hat?'

Mordecai's forehead puckered. 'I hope you'll give the workshops reasonable notice if you do decide to attempt that one.'

2

The workshops beside the Cavern of Mystery covered a larger area than the stage of the theatre itself. A carpenter's shop produced trick cabinets and trunks; there was a metalwork section for all kinds of supports, lifts, pulleys and pinions, and other machinery; and new uses for electricity, clarifying some things and, facilitating deception in others, were constantly being explored. One wall of the drawing office on the first floor was covered by a plan of the stage with trap doors and the sockets of various mechanisms marked. Strangers were banned from here as rigorously as from the backstage secrets. Further along the first floor, well away from the hammering and sawing and clatter of the main workshops, was the smaller room in which fine mechanisms were made. Here the automatic chess-player had been invented; here the controls of the famous dancing phantoms were serviced and timed at least once a fortnight; and here Caspian and Mordecai sometimes sat for hours on end concocting a score of new tricks and, on average, discarding nineteen.

Caspian placed announcements in *The Times* and the *Morning Post* to acquaint the public with the challenge he had issued and with the date of his special matinée.

Every morning he rehearsed with lazy tongs and rapping devices. As each new item emerged from the workshops Caspian devoted himself to mastering it, deliberately encouraging it to go wrong, then correcting the errors. One mistake on the day would be an invitation to the Chesterfields to pour scorn on his pretensions.

There was a full house for the matinée. None of the ushers had established whether the Chesterfields themselves were present, but they suspected that a few small groups, who had booked blocks of seats well in advance, were Chesterfield supporters, and they were ready for trouble.

The programme began with a speedy

review of some of the company's better-known tricks. The audience was impatient for the widely advertised 'Sixty Minutes with the Spirits' to begin, but the sheer speed and dexterity of the preliminaries quelled any hint of restlessness.

At last, to a fanfare from the orchestra pit, Count Caspar stepped forward and announced:

'Ladies and gentlemen, we now offer for your delectation a farrago of follies. You are welcome to laugh. You are meant to laugh. And I trust you'll continue to laugh when attending rival performances by those who claim to be moved — oh, so vigorously moved! — by insubstantial revenants.'

There was a sullen murmur from some parts of the auditorium; but it was too soon for the hecklers to strike.

'Every deceit you will witness this afternoon,' Caspar went on, 'is inspired by the deceits perpetrated on the public by this new breed of illusionists. We are grateful to them for providing so many amusing notions — but, unlike them, we claim no heavenly guidance. And there is of course no question of our infringing their copyright, for they themselves have sworn that it is not they but the spirits who perform . . . and the spirits are surely above such material considerations.'

A ripple of laughter ran across the stalls. The orchestra began to play very softly and dreamily.

'And now may I ask for the services of three unbiased members of the audience? I want four gentlemen to volunteer as observers, here on stage, of the phenomena that I shall produce. One of these four has already approached me. The others are invited to step forward.'

There was the usual hiatus. Nobody moved. Then a man came from the wings and stood by the circular table in the centre of the stage. At once there was a jeer from the centre stalls. 'He's one of your own! It's a sham!'

'On the contrary. This gentleman has gallantly offered his services because he is in a unique position to compare one set of manifestations with the other. He was present at a séance given by Mr. and Miss Chesterfield which I also attended.'

'Placed there by you then — and now.'

'Mr. Bellamy had never met me until our mutual visit to Russell Square. He has sworn an affidavit to that effect, which may be inspected in the foyer at the end of this performance. And the three others?' Count Caspar stood at the top of the steps leading up to the stage. 'If anyone is so minded as to challenge the integrity of our next three volunteers, I shall be glad to accept substitutes.'

The first three men who made for the stage were halted by a chorus of catcalls. One after another was challenged, until they retreated resentfully to their seats. It took some persuasion from Count Caspar to coax another three to come forward. When someone shouted a challenge to the third volunteer, the audience grew restless and there was a brief scuffle at the back of the stalls, Finally a substitute walked briskly down the aisle and up the steps, provoking no challenge whatsoever.

Almost certainly, thought Alexander Caspian, one of the Chesterfield contingent. Now he would need to be doubly skilful.

He turned his attention to the four-man committee and seated them around the table. Then he laid two wooden-rimmed skates before one of the men and said: 'Please inspect these two slates. Is there any mark upon them?'

The man vouched that there was not. Count Caspar turned both faces of each slate towards the other three, but made a point of not noticing an attempted grab made by the one he suspected of being an enemy. He put a stub of chalk on one slate, and covered it with the other; the wooden rims provided just enough space to accommodate the chalk.

'At the end of our sitting,' he said. 'Spirit fingers will have written a message in there. We will have it magnified so that the whole audience may see — and without looking at it I will tell you exactly what is written.'

He produced two thick rubber bands and asked that the two slates should be secured together.

'And now, sir — you sir — will you keep this beside your chair for the entire séance? Make sure it is not removed

— not even by an astral visitor.'

Two assistants came forward to blind-fold the sitters, so that they felt themselves in a room as dark as that in which séances generally took place.

'Are we all comfortable?' Count Caspar settled between two of the committee. 'Let us link hands.' He laid one hand on that of the man to his right, and on that of the man to his left. He had contrived that the probable mischief-maker sat on the far side of the table.

For a moment he let nerve and muscle go limp; then timed the flow of energy throbbing back, building up to a peak.

The sitters were in an imposed blackness. For the spectators the stage was bathed in light. It was rare for the Cavern of Mystery to reveal the mechanics of its magic, but for once Count Caspar wanted the public to see every-thing.

In full view of gods and groundlings he apported a bouquet of paper roses and brushed it past a sitter's ear; floated a tambourine above their heads with lazy tongs, and tapped them in passing with the lightness of a feather. While they were distracted by this rustling and rattling he carefully extracted his left foot from its shoe, magnetically clamped to the floor and still touching his neighbour's shoe. Flexing his big toe he made it crack, and intoned: 'Is there anyone there?'

'There's me up here,' shouted a wag from the gallery.

As laughter flowed and ebbed, Caspar began to drone questions: 'Rap twice for yes, once for no.' He stuck his leg well out so that the audience could see the twitching of his toe and hear the answering clicks and cracks. After a sequence of questions and answers he slid his foot back under the table and under the nearest claw of its central leg. He pressed upwards to make it rock.

The table refused to budge.

Again he thrust against the claw. There was a faint wobble, no more.

The man sitting opposite must know the method — as a Chesterfield employee he assuredly would — and was applying his own foot as a brake, making it impossible to shift the table more than a laborious inch. In a matter of seconds the audience would suspect there had been a hitch and would grow restive. There was only one thing for it. Caspar twisted his leg awkwardly to one side and managed to get his bare foot under the adjoining claw. At this angle the fretted woodwork bit painfully across his bare flesh. He jerked, and the table lurched. One false move and he could twist his ankle. He braced himself and, before his opponent could regain control, set the table rocking violently to and fro. Hands slid across the polished surface. With a bright light beamed on him, Caspar showed how to utilize this confusion by dragging together the right hand of the sitter on his left, the left hand of the man on his right, and, without their realizing it, freeing his own right hand and clamping his left down across both theirs. Each still felt the pressure of fingers and believed the circle to be still unbroken.

With his free hand he drew an umbrella spoke from the seam of his trouser leg, probed out towards the slates propped against a chair leg, and made a scraping, scratching noise against the outer side of one slate.

'At this point I'd like to ask the committee if the sensations they experience are the same as in a vauntedly genuine séance, or if they can detect any trickery.'

'Can't make out what's going on, and that's the truth.'

'Puts the wind up me a bit.'

Mr. Bellamy said: 'I can tell no difference between what went on with the Chesterfield twins and what goes on here.'

'It's simple.' The fourth man put his blindfolded head back and shouted for the audience's benefit. 'All those taps on our heads, it's simple: lazy tongs. Getting his feet out of his boot — there's a magnet, that's what it is, a magnet holding the boot to the floor. Old-fashioned trickery, all of it.'

'Hear, hear,' bellowed a claque from the circle.

Caspar nodded. 'So you know all the tricks? I'm most obliged to you. That confirms my belief: your spiritualist mediums are fellow magicians, using devices similar to my own. I applaud their skill — but not their spirituality.'

There was a patter of clapping, swelling to drown the abuse from the claque.

Caspar reclaimed his left shoe and stood up.

'We must dim the lights now, or you will not enjoy the full effect of our next visitors from beyond.'

Assistants brought a huge crystal ball on to the stage, complete with a tripod and a leather saucer in which to rest. As the lights went slowly down, Caspar went from one sitter to another, removing the blindfolds. His committee pushed their chairs a little way back from the table, and all watched the globe. Caspar settled himself on a chair some distance away with his hands folded in his lap and his eyes closed.

'I feel intimations from the other side,' he chanted.

A pinpoint of light in the heart of the crystal ball began to expand.

'My guide is close. Is there a message?'

Shapes began to swirl in the hazy globe.

'There is someone here you wish to speak to?'

The luminescent fog thinned. A face, distorted by the curvature, spread out until it seemed wrapped over the whole surface visible to the audience. It was a man's face, eyes slanted and chin pulled down over the glass to vanishing point.

'But that's me!' exploded Mr. Bellamy. 'Doctor . . . I mean, Count Caspar . . . where the deuce did you get that old photograph?'

'You?' said Caspar in mock concern. 'Oh, dear me. This will never do. Summoning up someone who isn't even dead yet!' He waited for laughter to subside, and went on in his normal voice: 'But thank you, Mr, Bellamy. I just wanted to show that cool planning makes it possible to get any amount of advance information — and material.'

The picture faded, to be replaced by that of a girl clad in wispy draperies, holding out imploring arms, falling into a sad dance and at last drifting away into nothingness.

There was a gasp from the audience. Watching the ethereal dance in the crystal ball, they had not noticed what was happening to Count Caspar. As light faded within the globe, it intensified around the magician. A phantom shape was beginning to extrude from his right hip. It grew slowly, shaking and rearing up and outwards, taking on fresh lineaments, growing a ghostly arm, turning against Caspar's shoulder and suddenly forming itself a head.

A woman screamed.

All the house lights blazed up, the stage was flooded with brightness again, and Caspar rose to his feet. The ectoplasmic phantom collapsed into a tangle of cheesecloth, which he caught under one arm and tossed towards the wings. At the same time, side curtains were drawn back to reveal the ingenious system of mirrors and the sylph-like girl dancing in the confined space between them, in line with the crystal ball.

'It's trickery! Falsification!'

The yell was drowned by laughter and applause, which continued as stagehands hurried on to move the crystal ball and set up a table reflector.

Caspar said: 'All magic is trickery. In

this theatre that has never been denied.'

Curtains at the back of the stage parted to reveal a large white screen.

'And now,' he said, 'shall we see what the spirits have written on the slates?' He leaned against the proscenium arch and allowed one of his assistants to blindfold him in turn. 'Perhaps one of our helpers will open the slates and place one — the one on which he will find writing — on the magnifier. I will then tell you what message was delivered from the shades,'

The wording would be magnified on the screen for the audience to read. He folded his arms across his chest, waiting for the rasp of the slate fitting into the reflector frame. When it was ready, the orchestra would play a C major chord.

He waited, ready to boom out the portentous slogan scrawled under the false surface.

The chord did not come. There was a ripple of uncertain amusement from the audience. At the same time the conductor of the orchestra tapped his baton twice, very lightly, against the edge of his rostrum: their standard signal that something had gone wrong. Usually a performer would then play for time. But the audience's reaction suggested that it was too late to extemporize: the damage, whatever it was, had been done.

The enemy must have switched slates. He had had the opportunity, and undoubtedly had the skill. So what was now written on the slate: what had been substituted for Caspar's own wording?

If his mentalist assistant had been planted in the stalls, they could have fallen into their number prompting routine. Though it would have conflicted with the pseudo-séance atmosphere, at least the gap could have been covered over. But they had not planned the trick that way, and it was too late now.

He tapped his brow and sketched a few histrionic passes in the air. The murmuring increased in volume.

Abruptly an incisive voice rose from the groundswell of uncertainty. In his head there rang, out of nowhere, the measured tones of Bronwen Powys, striking a response like the resonance of a finely cast bell.

Steadily and unequivocally she said: 'Count Caspar is a fraud and a blasphemer.'

He flinched. Then through her eyes he had a quite clear vision of the screen and its magnified message, as if seen from her seat in the circle.

He said: 'The spirits would appear to be favouring their loyal supporters this evening. The message, to whose sentiments I naturally do not subscribe, is . . . ' It took an effort to say the words aloud: ''Count Caspar is a fraud and a blasphemer'.'

Applause, bolstered suddenly by relief, was interrupted by further shouting.

'You couldn't have known!' He recognized the accents of Leon Chesterfield. 'That's just not possible. You didn't do that by scientific means. No, sir. Couldn't have.'

'Sit down,' came from somewhere at the back.

'That's no science. Not that. Magic — *black* magic, not fit for decent folk . . . '

'Be a good loser, man.'

Count Caspar removed his blindfold while a torrent of vilification flowed one way and then rolled back. Feelings for and against spiritualism ran high: he had realized that from the start, but had not expected quite such reactions.

'Ladies and gentlemen,' he began. A man stood up and clapped loudly to show his support. 'Ladies and gentlemen . . . ' It was a stentorian roar now. 'You have all seen how easy it is to conjure up spirits. If we have omitted any of your favourite phenomena, I apologize. And here and now I repeat the offer I've made before: I will donate one entire evening's receipts to any spiritualist who produces phenomena, which I cannot duplicate within seven days.'

He had come through unscathed, though the outcome was less happy than it might have been. He had not cheated his chosen antagonists; yet he could not explain the last-minute turning of the tables. Which meant that in a way he *had* cheated: he had not fulfilled his promise of defeating them by purely scientific means.

Brushing aside Louis Mordecai's congratulations and a stage hand's 'That was a close 'un, guv'nor', he went to his dressing room and slumped in a chair, trying to wipe his mind blank and ease his muscles. But there was a terrible admission he must first make.

Calling out into the void he implored Bronwen Powys to come and see him.

A few minutes later there was a tap at the door.

'Young lady, sir, says she knows you want to see her.'

She was wearing a velvety brown tunic and swathed skirt, with a gable hat peaked above her brow and those wide green eyes. Under her left arm she carried a slim black leather document case. Somehow they shook hands without touching.

Alexander Caspian let out a long breath. 'Thank you for extricating me once more from an awkward situation. I thought I was lost.'

'You were being tricked.'

'Outsmarted by experts. Admirable in their way. I should have been better prepared.'

'It takes two people,' she said, 'to read other minds accurately.' She smiled. 'And it's as well for the two of them to tune up before they start.'

She could reasonably have demanded an apology for his earlier dismissal of her claims. Instead, her smile was as easy and affectionate as if they were old, old friends who knew all about each other and could admit it and be content with it. He was about to make some conventional remark, then knew it would be superfluous.

Her face was above his shoulder as he turned to the mirror and dabbed at a smear of makeup, which had trickled from his temple during the heat of those last tense moments.

She said: 'You sent for me.'

'I . . . knew you were in the building. I could hardly let you slip away without . . . ' His eyes met hers in the glass.

His dark, almost gipsy features came from his mother's side of the family, as did the flowing, cajoling gestures that counted for so much in his professional career. Often at the crucial moment of some painstakingly rehearsed illusion, when it was essential to divert the audience's attention from what was really happening, he would recognize in some spontaneous flourish the turn of his mother's wrist or the coaxing curve of her arm. Descendant of a once noble Transylvanian family, she had married a young Magyar who had left his border hills to study engineering and seek work in the Hungarian capital. They fled the country with Kossuth after the collapse of his nationalist campaigns, and settled in due course at Littleham in Devon. Alexander was born at Exmouth in 1855. His father had found employment in this country tidying up the mess left by Brunel's disastrous atmospheric railway experiment between Exeter, Teignmouth and Totnes, and working on the introduction of conventional steam trains across the county.

Alex's own education was begun by his mother, illumined by Slav and Magyar history and legend, and bubbling with several different languages. From his father he inherited an artificer's skills and a manual dexterity, which was to stand him in good stead. Fascinated by the intrinsic beauty of such small mechanisms as clock and watch movements, he was led on to an interest in telescopes and so to astronomy itself. While still at university he invented a new bearing for refractory telescopes. At London and Heidelberg he had been equally interested in the philosophical aspects of astronomy, mathematics and the cosmos, and after a final course in Prague was awarded a doctorate in philosophy.

Dining out, or among friends at his club, he preferred to talk about horses and the finer points of pugilism. If tempted to boast, it was less likely to be of his conjuring brilliance than of his early prowess with the foils: a duellist able to hold his own with the most arrogant Heidelberg had to offer, he emerged from all his bouts unscathed, regarding a duelling scar as a mark of incompetence rather than a token of virility. And gradually the threads of his talents were drawn inevitably together into one skein. Mechanical skills, physical fitness, a persuasive tongue, the movements of a dancer: they were all prerequisites of a prestidigitator, a master of legerdemain. What began as a hobby during college entertainment developed into a specialist's obsession with the sheer craftsmanship of illusion.

On the verge of embarking on an academic career, Caspian was tempted by two London friends to mystify larger audiences than he had so far known. Heirs to prosperous merchant banking families, they had a fancy to combine pleasure and profit by setting him up as manager and main attraction of a Cavern of Mystery in Leicester Square. It was an instant success. Critics marvelled and tried to explain away the marvels they witnessed. The general public was content to be dazzled without attempting to understand how the miracles were achieved. Alexander Caspian became Count Caspar and played to full houses night after night, week after week. Chained in a cage above the auditorium, he freed himself in three minutes. Locked and roped within a cabinet on stage, he reappeared in one of the upper boxes. Young women vanished at the flurry of his cloak, poultry and playing cards were plucked from the front rows of the stalls, and always there was a grand pageant or transformation scene to round off the performance.

After two years the strain began to tell. Such was the daily queue at the doors that Caspian had introduced matinées. Rival impresarios predicted that these would fail: there was no public demand for afternoon entertainments. They were wrong. But the toll was heavy. However assiduously one kept up a morning programme of physical exercise, sheer exhaustion threatened to pull one down. The first slip on stage would be a slip too many. An act bungled would be a dangerous crack in Count Caspar's reputation. Slowing his pace cautiously, the magician introduced other magicians. His theatre became the means of practising illusionists, vying with one another in the creation of new perplexities. There was no room for the second-rate at the Cavern of Mystery. Count Caspar guaranteed the quality of every performer on his stage; but was himself always the most powerful magnet, assuring a throng at the early doors, an admiring guard of honour at the stage door, and a congestion of carriages in the square.

Summing up his career as tersely and undemonstratively as possible for Bronwen Powys, he grew uncomfortably aware that she heard far more than he was saying: the more he tried to understate his achievements, the more she sensed of his private vanities. It was somehow essential that she should understand the forces that drove him: but only so much as he chose to let her understand.

She was smiling again. 'But your interest in real magic, as opposed to stage illusions . . . '

'*Real?*'

It was in all seriousness and in no attempt to contrive fresh sensations for his theatre that Alexander Caspian had set about investigating the manifestations of spiritualist mediums. There was not a salon in London that did not boast its regular visiting voice; not a fashionable home where séances were not held at least once a week, and puzzling spirit messages translated and earnestly discussed. He was curious. If there was another plane of existence, if such messages really did come through . . .

Anger took the place of curiosity. He heard bells rung behind his head and knew precisely how the effect was achieved; heard the solemn intonations of spirit guides and the rattling of tambourines; watched shadowy figures emerge from curtains and disappear before any hand could clutch them; and was furious. Bereaved families yearned to hear from dead loved ones; earnest researchers sought to establish contact with an afterworld from which great wisdom must surely be granted; and all were deceived.

Dr. Caspian became a member of a committee set up by the Royal Society to test psychic phenomena. He offered his advice and services free to the inquirers of the Dialectical Society and the newly established Society for Psychical Research. His abrasive scepticism was not always welcome, but it was difficult for an honest investigator to jib at the knowledgeable unmasking of falsehood. Until the dross was cleared away, there could be no accurate appraisal of whatever truth might lie beneath.

'If I can duplicate emanations by natural means,' Caspian repeatedly asserted, 'then we may reasonably assume there is nothing supernatural in the original emanations.'

In the role of Count Caspar he parodied Daniel Dunglas Home's celebrated feat of levitation. On other occasions he called voices out of hidden megaphones, instructed his orchestra to remain silent for five minutes while he provided his own musical accompaniment from ghostly trumpets and a concertina, and demonstrated how a medium involved in a current court case had fraudulently obtained money from a distinguished physicist, who ought to have known better, with mystical messages from his dead wife.

'But why should you be so personally concerned,' asked Bronwen Powys, 'with establishing materialistic solutions to everything?'

'I cannot bear to see what I know to be purely professional skills misused to deceive the gullible. Used not for admitted, entertaining deception, but to deceive people into believing there is no deception. The truth — '

'You acknowledge only one kind of truth?'

Caspian remembered a night, that one terrible night in Prague, when . . . But no. This was the thing he would not remember, must always refuse to remember; and far down in his mind must conceal from this young woman's far too candid mind. He had been ill that night years ago: ill, hysterical, light-headed as ascetics so often were from lack of food and lack of sleep.

Brusquely he changed the subject. 'What brings you to London?'

Her eyes questioned him for a dangerous moment. He concentrated on the lovely, proud set of her head, the skin with none of that blanched translucency so often found with auburn hair, and the promise of her lips — a promise around which she suddenly feinted and withdrew.

'I'm in London to buy some new equipment,' she said. 'I've already indulged in a portable binocular camera and an actinometer.'

'Indeed. An . . . ?'

'Actinometer. It helps in deciding exposure time — measures the intensity of light by a differential thermometer.'

Her eyes, he thought: the intensity of light in her eyes, and the rich and enriching light which burned so steadily through her whole being . . .

'To pay for it all I've sold a number of views to the London Stereoscopic Company, and some for diorama lantern slides. And' — she opened the document case and took out a sepia print — 'I felt I must drop in and see one of your performances. And bring you a present.'

She propped it against his dressing room mirror. It was the photograph of himself at Hexney, with the mysterious blur in the background touched out to sharpen the contour of his head.

'I'm not sure my father would have approved,' she said. 'He was a great exponent of naturalism. No patience with retouching. I carried this out simply as an experiment.'

Because, he thought, it marred her picture of me.

A flash of her eyes showed that she knew what she had given away.

'But don't we all do it,' said Caspian, 'all of the time? In every aspect of our life, forever tinting and retouching. We put in things which were not there originally, and gloss over blemishes we'd prefer not to be there.'

When we two speak, we veil what we know to be true. But what if we dared to speak nothing but truth?

He said: 'This gift of yours — '

'Of ours.'

It was still difficult for him to concede that he might be an adept in a craft he had so long denied. Trying to lessen its significance, he said lightly: 'I must admit it would be a considerable asset in a thought-reading scene.'

'You see it as nothing more than another stage illusion?'

'Hardly an illusion.'

'So you're admitting it was real? That there's a magic beyond mere conjuring tricks?'

He wanted to argue, yet not with her. Never before had he hesitated to accept a challenge. Now he knew that the challenge she offered was the most important he had ever encountered, and he was afraid: not physically, but in a deep recess of his soul.

'This telepathy . . . ' The performance and its hazards had drained him of energy. 'I know one thing,' he said. 'One very important thing.'

'And what would that be?'

'We must meet again while you are in London. Soon. When we can talk at greater length.'

She smiled. 'You mean when you have talked yourself back into scepticism?'

3

A chill October afternoon bleached the front-age of Buckingham Palace and the towers and turrets of Whitehall. A black carriage and black horses proceeded at a funereal pace down the Mall. In St. James's Park a duck, flicking one wing, wedged itself more securely under the bank and sent unadventurous ripples across the lake. Branches and a few rusty leaves were brittle against the sky. Sounds fell hard and sullen, oddly without echo. Only within the minds of the two looking down from the bridge into leaden sky reflected in leaden water was there a gentle, continuing resonance.

Caspian said: 'You spoke the other day of minds needing to tune up before they could read others. When you reached me in the theatre, how difficult was it for you to convey a message to a mind as unreceptive as mine?'

'You're not unreceptive.' Her elbows on

the rail, Bronwen touched gloved fingers together. 'Determined to sing in a different key, that's all.'

'I wish only to be sure that the sirens' songs are not too misleading.'

A young couple came on to the bridge with a child toddling between them, her gloved hands clutching theirs. The little girl squeaked some meaningless words and the mother smiled fondly down. As they passed, Bronwen not merely lowered her voice but instinctively let her thoughts take up the conversation and invited Caspian to join her. Instead, a message from outside spilled across their minds, blotting out everything else.

If I could push them over, drown them both, be done with them. Or if they could disappear, just somehow cease to exist.

The little girl nuzzled her father's hand with her cheek.

I don't think I can go on much longer, not like this.

Bronwen and Caspian were presented with a picture of a cramped parlour: chenille curtains, a piano, a brass tabletop on folding legs, and brass fire irons. The fire irons grew larger, the husband was reaching for a poker and raising it . . .

Then the three were past, side by side, the wife making some everyday remark, which faded into the distance.

Without needing to exchange even a confirmatory glance, Caspian and Bronwen moved away from the rail and began to walk slowly along the path.

Aloud she said: 'It won't happen, will it?'

'It may. If pressures become unbearable, it may.'

'But we mustn't let it.'

'We don't know that it *will* happen. Only that it *could*.'

'If we can so clearly sense a crime in the making, there must be some way of averting it.'

'Drawing it away from the fire before it comes to the boil?' He clicked his tongue doubtfully. 'I can imagine the young man's face if we accused him of harbouring murderous daydreams. There must be thousands of cases like his, where the fantasy is the only way of warding off the reality.'

'But oughtn't we to investigate, to discover when there's a danger of it becoming reality?'

'Are we proposing, then, to set up a psychic detective agency?'

'I don't know what we're proposing. Or what's proposing itself to us.'

Such a short time ago he would have lectured her on the follies of palmists and soothsayers, on — what was it? Unscientific conclusions drawn from inadequate evidence. Now he did not dare. All he could say was:

'Have we the right to pry into other people's minds?'

Or into our own?

They both asked it. Nobody observing them strolling so staidly in the park would have glimpsed more than the slight sparkle in Bronwen's eye, a half-protesting turn of her head.

Breathlessly she said: 'It would be impossible. Quite insufferable to have no secrets — no private world.'

Caspian looked away from her, and still saw every feature of her elusive yet enticing face. Impossible, she said; and of course she was right. Every tradition demanded certain formalities taken at a certain well-regulated pace. Social conduct was no artificial device: it had the logic of music, mathematics, and civilization. A personable man and a comely young lady wishing to test their mutual emotions knew the innate good sense of conventional measures, nicely balanced between protection and provocation: steps and preenings as strictly prescribed as those of birds and animals in their courting dances, displaying finery and fluffing up feathers — skimming fingertips, as it were, first gloved and then uncovered, advancing and coyly retreating, allowing flirtation to develop according to an urbane timetable. But he and Bronwen Powys, on such slight acquaintance, had gone dizzyingly far beyond those proprieties — without having any clear idea of the distance they might yet be carried.

He saw her; and turned to see her in reality; and saw the face of a stranger. Yet he had only to think of the mouth of that stranger to know what her lips would feel like against his, what the touch of her cheek would be like — and to know that these thoughts had brought that flush to her cheek.

'Sir, you're going too far.'

'Haven't we both gone far beyond the conventional parries and courtesies?'

'You have no right to . . . to eavesdrop.'

'I'm still stumbling, Miss Powys,' he said aloud, and secretly said *Bronwen* and knew that she heard him. 'I do not yet have my bearings.'

'There's a children's game: they spy — '

'The fourth bush from the far end of the bridge,' he replied without hesitation.

She quickened her step as if to escape him. Automatically he framed a plea to delay her, and she laughed back over her shoulder. 'You're accepting that there are forces beyond your scientific calculations?'

He caught her up. 'Given time, I'll work it out.'

We will turn along the path near the Horse Guards Parade and sit on the second seat from this end.

Obeying her before it had occurred to him to protest, he slowed at the intersection of paths and automatically took the right fork.

They settled facing the great deserted quadrangle. A faint puff of cold wind stirred a flurry of dust.

Would she object to his smoking a cigar?

She said immediately: 'Perhaps you'll sit on my other side, so that the smoke blows away from me.'

What shall we do? How far may we safely go?

'Safety could be another name for complacency,' he said.

Her mind touched his and darted away. He tried to catch her. She conjured up for his benefit a vision of a clipped privet hedge, which became a maze, and in the middle of it she raised a mocking head and cried a message he could not hear but which would be revealed to him when he reached her. They began to play a game of mental tig. She dodged, he brushed her with eager fingers, she pouted and was gone. Mock severe, he accused her of being a witch. 'That's not fair!' she said aloud when his hand stroked her neck though they still sat decorously, a few feet apart, staring at the barren parade ground.

He tapped an inch of cigar ash to the ground and said: 'If we could learn how to turn this faculty on and off, we could open up the most time-saving short cuts. In scientific research, in committee work — even in my own theatre . . . '

'I doubt that it's amenable to that kind of discipline.'

'All natural forces can sooner or later be tamed. That's how every human advance has been made. We've learnt to use fire, the winds, electricity — '

'You're so stubborn,' she said. 'So earthbound.'

'It's a good place to keep one's feet.'

So delightful. She said it secretly, but betrayed it in the twinkling of a feline eye.

Aloud she said: 'The clearest messages come if you let your mind wander.'

He thought of his early career, when he had perfected an act of juggling six plates and simultaneously managing a somersault every ten seconds. One had to learn not to let one's mind wander. She would not appreciate the difficulty of unlearning such a thing.

It was too cold to sit still any longer. They got up together, again without consultation, and walked on together.

'This talent must obey natural laws,' he said, 'as everything else does.'

Teasingly she implanted in his mind a picture of herself racing across the grass towards the water, and he very nearly ran after her. But she was still beside him.

She said: 'Can't you accept the possibility of mediums — genuine mediums — who collect fragments out of thin air without knowing what they're hearing? Perhaps responding to unconscious longings in the minds of their sitters?'

He shook his head, but then grudgingly conceded: 'There may be some electromagnetic forces we've not yet analysed. Or some sort of sound impulses we produce above or below the range of normal hearing. Laboratory tests might — '

'Let go,' she cried. 'Let yourself drift, instead of clinging so tightly. When we walk' — she exaggerated her stride, swishing her skirt about her ankles — 'we don't supervise our feet going one in front of the other. We just walk. And this telepathy — when it happens, it just happens. Isn't that enough for you?'

He shook his head. 'No.'

'So pedantic! And to think that when we first met I thought of you . . . '

She pretended to be distracted by a bird flying up to a blackened branch. He tried to snatch an unspoken admission, but she had already rushed up her defences. He had to ask: 'How did you think of me?'

'As a part of those odd goings-on in Hexney. Maybe of causing them!'

'How could I possibly . . . '

'When we were there, in that atmosphere, it was hard to know what belonged and what didn't.'

They shared a sudden vision of Hexney, of the footprints, of twisted bushes on the edge of illimitable fen. Fear struck out from her. He caught his breath. At the extremity of the park they came to a halt, lapped by the noise of hoofs and wheels and the occasional crack of a whip from Trafalgar Square. But briefly London ceased to exist.

He said: 'What is it that frightens you?

What's your own special nightmare?'

This time she held nothing back. Her mind opened to him as if to purge childhood and adult terrors in one confessional outburst.

'Eels?' he said. 'Fish?' She flinched, yet let him probe further. *Things*, he detected, in deep marshes. *The nameless?* But there was nothing without a name: or nothing for which one could not devise a name, a classification. 'No worse than spiders, slugs, beetles,' he said. 'Messy, but not so very frightening.'

She shuddered, not from feminine squeamishness but from an ancient intuitive horror of writhing and multiplying coils, of something that embraced her and slithered over her arms and her belly in a hideous intercourse of warm flesh and cold slime.

'If you can make me feel like that,' said Caspian, 'when there are only the two of us here, what could a mob of believers be made to feel by . . . by whatever their belief was?'

We must return to Hexney. It is demanded of us,

The declaration was clamorous, touched off consciously by neither of them. He stared at the traffic and willed London to be restored to its proper dimensions.

Beside him, a furtive little man with ragged shoes edged closer, as if to cross the road when they did. They caught his impulses between their own converging thoughts.

'I wouldn't advise either,' said Caspian.

'Eh? Speakin' to me, guv'nor?'

'Yes. To you. I was saying that I would not advise you either to pick my pocket or attempt a surreptitious opening of this lady's reticule.'

The man's jaw dropped, but no protest would come. He stared with mounting apprehension at Caspian, then dashed across the road, narrowly avoiding death under the offside wheel of a smart speeding gig.

Bronwen said: 'I'm not sure we should meet again. It would be safer for both of us to stay apart. Far apart. Together, we hear too much.'

'We're only at the beginning.'

'When we talked about retouching

photographs, you said we survived only by the use of disguise and polite falsifications. Is it safe to abandon those comforts?'

'That's what we shall discover.'

'No disguises? No reservations?'

'One would have to agree — '

'Two would have to agree.'

'Two would have to agree,' Caspian accepted, 'on certain demarcation lines, beyond which there could be no trespassing.'

'That's asking for a great deal of mutual trust.'

'More than in most . . . ' He had been about to say 'marriages'. She heard him and looked wonderingly at him.

They crossed the road.

When they set foot on the opposite kerb she mischievously invoked for him a panorama of Welsh mountains in place of the white terrace ahead. He stumbled, then banished it and said:

'You're not going home? Not yet?'

'I've done what I came to do. And a pretty penny it's cost me. I can't afford to stay longer in London.'

'For a few more days, though. There's still so much to discuss. So much we have no right to shirk.' When she did not reply he asked humbly, yet with a fatalistic assurance: 'May I visit you on your own ground?' He would come to Caernarvon and stay at a local hotel and they would go on talking: aloud when necessary, silently when they had explored the possibilities — and the dangers.

'My theatre's always closed at the beginning of November,' he explained, 'while we prepare a special Christmas season.'

'You've already deserted it once this year, to visit Hexney. Can you be spared again?'

'Some excellent magicians stood in for me last time. This time I can safely leave my experts to prepare what ordeals they choose for me. They'll enjoy it.'

To visit Hexney. The shadow crept out and fell across them.

She said: 'It won't leave us alone.'

'Together we might solve the mystery, when we are ready.'

'You mean that as soon as you reach

Wales you want me to — '

'I mean that we shall go,' he said, 'when it pleases us to go. Not when Hexney demands it. It's one of the things to discuss. On your own ground,' he repeated, 'Miss Powys.'

In your mind you don't call me Miss Powys.

In my heart I call you Bronwen.

She said: 'I hardly know you.'

Silently he called her a liar, and she took his arm and did not even pretend to rebuke him.

4

The west wind blew a fine drizzle against the massive bulwarks of Caernarvon Castle and relentlessly down the grey stone streets. Bronwen moved a table closer to the window to get a better light as she sorted through her most recent sets of prints and pencilled a catalogue reference on the back of each.

In the middle of the morning Ceinwen, the maid Mrs. Lewis Jones had found to replace the defecting Eiluned, came to ask if she would be needed for an hour, as she wanted to do a little bit of shopping so that she could take something up the valley to her mother on Sunday afternoon. She bobbed her thanks when Bronwen told her to take a couple of hours if she needed them, and her eyes strayed nervously to the shelves and racks and the pictures of gaunt buildings laid out upon the table.

Ceinwen was a plump, bovine little

thing, a chapel-goer and a tidy seamstress who to Bronwen appeared at all times, literally and metaphorically, to be keeping her elbows tight in to her sides. Edging along the row of pictures she nodded respectfully at each one, but did not speak until she glimpsed a print set aside from the others. Putting her head on one side, she looked down into Alexander Caspian's features.

'Someone you know, miss?'

Bronwen coloured. It was absurd of her to keep that picture always to hand, placed where she could glance at it from time to time as she worked: as if a glimpse every ten or fifteen minutes would bring him closer, hurrying the time of his arrival!

'A good-looking gentleman, now, isn't he?' Then, deciding that her allotted time on this subject was up and that she might already have gone too far, Ceinwen hastened away.

Bronwen pushed the photograph under a heap of papers and tried to pretend it was not there as she went on classifying prints and cataloguing them as she had so often and so repetitively done before. But

Caspian would not be so summarily dismissed. Until recently it had seemed that her father still stood at her shoulder commenting and criticizing. Now Alexander Caspian had taken his place. She saw through his eyes and heard his bantering tone within her head — and, more insidiously, that serious tone of his as they parted.

'It will be difficult' — he might have been leaning over her now, his breath warm against her ear — 'keeping the barriers secure, keeping our promises.'

'Unless we live a thousand miles apart.'

'A prospect I'm unwilling to contemplate. Even then we might experiment with transmitting messages at long range. But I think distance and intervening mental cross-currents would provide too many obstacles.'

She attempted it now, like a telegraphist sending a message and waiting for the tap of a reply. There was nothing. She felt insecure; incomplete.

Mrs. Lewis Jones brought in the second post. There were two trade advertisements, and an envelope from London.

Although she had seen Caspian's handwriting only aslant, in his notebook jottings at Hexney, she recognized it at once.

He wrote to say that he could not immediately set out for Caernarvon. Shortly after she left London he had received a command to perform at Sandringham in Norfolk for the Prince and Princess of Wales — 'To keep His Royal Highness away from the gaming tables or Newmarket for a few hours, I fancy' — and feared it might be high treason to disobey such a royal summons.

Walking along the town walls in the afternoon to clear her head, Bronwen felt both impatience and relief. She had been so sure he would soon be with her. Looking out across the wind-ruffled channel towards Anglesey and back at the wintry hills she saw nothing and nobody but Caspian. Then there came a menacing shadow at his shoulder; and behind him, clearer and more solid than mountain or shadow, were the square and lanes of Hexney. By now the footprints must be off the drove road and up the lane, closing in on the marketplace. About this at least she could be glad: they would not now be going back there — if they were to return to the place at all, it could not be until after the night of Guy Fawkes and whatever else might be present. Not I, she thought. Not until it's all over, and he's with me.

That night she dreamed. She had tried shamelessly to lull herself into a mood of dreaming about Caspian. In the mental dissociation of sleep, desires ranged more freely and to the receptive mind there might come such messages as those which rose unbidden in the consciousness of bewildered mediums. She turned on her pillow and murmured Caspian's name.

He did not come. Instead she caught the fleeting movements of a girl in Hexney, that girl who had been caught up in the dance. What was her name? Carrie, that was it: Carrie, who had tried to involve her, tried to force a stone on her.

All at once she was being showered with stones, and she was back in the bedrooms of The Griffin. They did not hurt her but flew slowly, giving her time to dodge in and out; and one curled in through the window as if lobbed by a skilled juggler, over the sill and into the room and silently down into a corner of her case, lying open and ready for last-minute packing.

At breakfast she said: 'Mrs. Lewis, will you show Ceinwen where we keep the luggage in the box-room, and get her to bring my blue case down, please?'

Ten minutes later Ceinwen carried the case into the breakfast room. The house-keeper's inquiring face floated across the gap in the doorway as she reluctantly closed the door and went away.

Bronwen opened the case. She had half expected it to rattle as she moved it, but there was no sound. She prodded the lining, then pulled open one of the silk, padded pockets.

A stone the size of a small dumpling lay tucked away in the bottom of the pocket.

She could not believe that it had been there when she unpacked. That it might have fallen into her case and into the pocket during that shower of stones was feasible; but that she should have unpacked, here in Caernarvon, and not noticed . . . ?

Ceinwen watched her curiously. 'What is it, miss?'

Bronwen took out the stone. The box-room was cold at the best of times, and the lining of the case had been cold when her fingers brushed against it. But the stone was as warm as if it had been resting on a hob beside the fire, and as her palm closed round it she felt it begin to throb.

It could not have been an accident. No random poltergeist mischief. There had been the flurry of a skirt, glimpsed on the corner. Carrie Lavater. The flight of one stone guided — by what force, what skill?

I will let go, she said to herself. I will drop it.

She could not.

All she could do was force her hand open a fraction, to look at the strange scratches and whorls on the surface of the stone. Like runic writing. Casting the runes . . . transferring a curse from one person to another.

Ceinwen was holding her hand out.

'What is it, miss?'

But she must not give it to the girl. Or to any other girl. Throw it away? No. Whoever picked it up might be snared in whatever wickedness had been set upon it.

Superstitious nonsense. Was that Caspian's voice, or only her wish that it should be Caspian's voice?

She clung to the stone, burning itself into her flesh.

'Ceinwen, we must pack.'

'Where we going then, miss? If we're to go away, I'll have to tell me mam.'

'Only for a few days,' said Bromven. 'Into the country. Not to the big bad city.'

'Where, then, miss?'

'A little place called Hexney.'

The girl's milky face went paler. 'Oh, now, I couldn't be doing that. Not that place, no. There's impossible that is.'

'What's got into you, Ceinwen?'

'I'm sorry, miss, but after what I've heard I wouldn't fancy it, indeed.'

'You've been listening to that wretched Eiluned Edwards.'

'Awful it sounded and no mistake.'

Awful, and no mistake. The stone throbbed its implacable summons.

⋆   ⋆   ⋆

On the lake two swans described slow parabolas that would not disturb the beauty of their own reflections, nudging proud breasts through the trailing remnants of departed summer's water lilies. A gardener swept up the fallen leaves of a venerable oak and whistled tunelessly up the slope towards the terrace.

Professor Murray said: 'A touch of dank Norfolk air doesn't come amiss after the heat of your conjurations last evening, Doctor.'

'I'm sorry you feared being set on fire,' said Caspian.

'The most impressive part was the Amphitrite illusion. I lay awake for some time trying to analyse your methods. You'll not divulge them, I suppose?'

'And make you the success of Cambridge dinner parties?'

'Academic interest only, I assure you.'

'His Royal Highness took a more than

academic interest in my card tricks. He has already hinted to me that a few private lessons wouldn't come amiss.'

'You'll be a peer of the realm yet, Dr. Caspian.'

'I prefer to remain a private seer of the realm.'

The professor winced. 'I endure enough of that sort of thing from my undergraduates, sir.'

They strolled up the grass towards the tangled gables, turrets and chimneys of Sandringham House. Caspian had been subjected to many strictures on the flamboyance of his own Cavern of Mystery, with its minarets and meaningless domes; but really, the absurdity of this skyline was second to none — and without theatrical excuse. Still, it was vastly enjoyable; as the hospitality had been.

'The most entertaining part of the evening,' Caspian said in all sincerity, 'was your disquisition on those strange focal points of Danish pagan history and legend.'

'You flatter me.'

'No. I simply want to know more.

From where I was sitting, it was difficult to catch all you were saying to the Princess of Wales.'

'A fascinating audience, Her Royal Highness.'

'You were discussing her homeland. She was not just fascinating but fascinated.'

'Ah, yes. Gallehus. I'm afraid the hospitality went to my head. I held forth rather pompously about relationships between Danish and Anglian burial grounds, and . . . oh, dear, I did hold forth, did I not?'

'Brilliantly,' said Caspian. 'I lured you out here this afternoon to see if you could be stimulated to continue. Gallehus,' he prompted.

'The very word echoes, don't you think? As it has echoed down the centuries. A very strange place, Doctor. Very strange.' The professor smiled the deferential smile common to all scholars about to pretend diffidence about their favourite subject. 'There it is, no more than a bleak hamlet on the bleakest of Jutland levels; yet over the centuries it has

253

attracted the most violent storms and has been struck over and over again by lightning, always on the same spot. Then in the seventeenth century a magnificent golden horn was found in a field — and another one a hundred years later. They dated from the early sixth century, and must have represented a large part of the gold existing in the country at the time. Why had they been buried?'

'To accompany some great chieftain into the next world?' Caspian suggested.

'Even the greatest chieftain in the land would not have been worthy of such extravagance. And we know of no such chieftain, in any case. It's more likely that they were part of some awesome ceremony at the changeover from the Old Religion to that of the Nordic deities. Zodiacal signs and some strange animal and sub-human figures on the horns would seem to bear this out.'

'The gold itself would hardly have attracted lightning.'

'No. But there can be little doubt that something did — that it's a place fraught with some inexplicable significance.'

'You believe, then, in places on which supernatural forces are concentrated at certain times in history?'

'As a historian, Doctor, I record and collate and deduce. Belief is another matter. Until I'm positive that records are complete, I hold back from generalization.'

'Gallehus is one mysterious place. Do you know of anything similar in our own country? Anywhere not far from Sandringham for example?' When Murray did not at once reply, Caspian added: 'Hexney, say?'

They came up beside a wall sprouting withered tufts of grey hair-grass, and turned along the lime walk. There was no wind and although the day was cool it was not so sharp as to hurry their tread.

'You know of Hexney,' said Murray with a tinge of wariness.

'I spent some days there recently. Investigating the footprints. You've heard of the footprints?'

'Vague tales reached Cambridge. A few esoteric jokes flowered at high table recently.'

'And you were not curious enough to follow up the jokes?'

'My dear Dr. Caspian, who in this world has the time to follow up even one tenth of the more delectable rumours he hears? But' — they paced on — 'do please recount your own impressions. Those who know the place at all give the impression that it's . . . well, a place best not tampered with.'

Caspian briskly summarized his experiences, selecting only what was strictly relevant to the professor's own theme. This was no time or place for introducing a third party to the mutual secrets which he and Bronwen had still not unravelled to their own satisfaction. He concentrated on what he had heard and theorized about the history of plague and fire, and of the significance of the Harvest Gathering and Bonfire Night. He was embarking on some careful speculations about the footprints when it dawned on him that Murray had virtually ceased to listen. Throughout his comments on the history of the village, the professor's head had hunched lower between his shoulders as if he were being given some deplorably inept paraphrase of a lecture he had recently delivered. One waited for an explosion, a putting to rights. Now, unable to keep it pent up any longer, he burst out:

'But that's not the real Hexney story at all. Not at all.'

'In London I went to the trouble of verifying what was known. Little enough, in all conscience, but it tallied.'

'Not the real facts,' Murray insisted. 'We have certain documents in Trinity. Not often consulted. And for most researchers, best left alone. His Royal Highness has some interesting local material in his library here, too. Disturbing stuff, all of it, if you believe that children inherit not just the punishment for the sins of their fathers unto seven generations, but also a penchant for the sins themselves.'

There was still no breeze, but staring to the east Caspian felt an icy dart striking at him across the park from unseen washlands and, beyond, the unsheltered fens.

He said: 'What is this damned Hexney? A centre . . . a hub of forces . . . ? What do you know about it that I should learn?'

'Perhaps you had better know nothing.'

Caspian was as capable as his companion of high indignation. He stopped, and drew himself up, towering over the professor.

Murray said: 'I'm sorry, Doctor. You are of course the best judge. Having gone so far, we can hardly dismiss the matter. I will tell you what I remember.'

They went on a little way and reached a plinth supporting an eyeless marble bust. The professor set his haunches against its rim, and for a moment studied his laced-up boots. When he began to speak he was solemn and reluctant but soon warmed to his subject.

'Eastern England has been blemished with a number of what one might almost call fever spots. Repeatedly breaking out in religious troubles, political, social troubles — and yet with something deeper than that. Places, some of them, so contaminated, as it were, that they'll never cease to exude poison. And side by side with them are the strongholds of other dissidents — men of good will, men turning their backs on the corruption of cities and seeking for truth in loneliness. My own university was founded in a damp and forbidding region by philosophers who wished to attract only the most austere idealists. Those who mistrusted them declared it a land of hobgoblins and heathens. And to be honest,' said Professor Murray, 'so it was — and is.'

He pushed himself upright, took Caspian's arm, and led him along the house, back towards the lime walk, telling his tale in measured tones, with an occasional declamatory thrust of his right index finger towards the heavens

'When those who had fled from Bloody Mary's persecutions returned, many had been influenced by cults and practices which even Mary's successor could hardly have been expected to approve. Large numbers settled in the waterlogged fens and found many kindred spirits who had remained and secretly practised ancient rituals. But at the same time there were other exiles who had passed their time under Calvin's influence, with their mentor's hatred of witches and rival sects burnt into their brains. Those of them who chose the eastern counties as their abode were soon ravenous for the tracking down of witch cults and the old rites.

'Some hereabouts regard Oliver Cromwell as one of our more distinguished heroes. But a part of his family fortune derived from his grandfather's accusation of witchcraft against a hapless local woman whom he helped send to the gallows thereafter acquiring all her property. Well into the last century we had an annual sermon preached at Queen's College against the sin of witchcraft and enchantments, paid for from Cromwell's proceeds. It's a region echoing with such trickeries and persecutions — and with the reasons for such persecution.'

'No more than echoes?'

Murray steered him into the house. There were two libraries side by side in the eastern corner, their high windows looking out upon a vault of sky and the superb avenue of lime trees.

'His Royal Highness most graciously allows me the run of his collection.' Murray reached down a volume. 'A fine section devoted to county histories and documents. Several items greatly coveted by the Fitzwilliam.' He found a page and set the book on a table, one thumb pressed down to keep it open.

Caspian leaned over the page.

'May it please Your Grace to understand that witches and sorcerers within these few years are marvellously increased within Your Grace's realm. Your Grace's subjects pine away even unto the death; their colour fadeth, their flesh rotteth, their speech is benumbed, their senses are bereft . . .'

'Thus the Bishop of Salisbury,' said Murray, 'urging Queen Elizabeth to be more severe. He persuaded her to issue laws stamping out 'fantastical and devilish practices' of the Old Religion. And her successor introduced a fine retinue of Scottish cranks who set about persecution with a will.' Murray closed the book and set another in its place. 'Here we come to the activities of the deplorable Matthew Hopkins in East Anglia — self-styled Witchfinder-General, cheered on by the Puritans. Responsible for the deaths of hundreds of old women and no small number of men. Elizabeth had never officially authorized the use of torture in obtaining confessions; James and his boggart-ridden minions tacitly encouraged it; but Hopkins gloated over it. Like his German counterparts in the Bamberg and Nuremberg scares, he believed that supposed witches should be 'tortured so thin that the sun will shine through them'.'

Caspian narrowed his eyes to decipher the ornate script. There was a note of Hopkins' having visited Hexney and subjected three women to the water test, one drowning and therefore being proclaimed innocent of sorcery, the other two floating and receiving the death penalty. Hopkins' account book, most scrupulously kept, duly noted receipt of the statutory twenty shillings a head for such deeds.

Through the musty smell of old books

and papers there penetrated a noisome tang of undying wickedness.

'And as for Hexney's local festivals . . . '

Professor Murray drew a large leather-bound tome with a stained white spine from the lowest shelf and lifted it to the table. A puff of dust rose from its crinkled pages as he opened it and drew up a chair for Caspian.

'Some of this was hastily scribbled by an anonymous survivor, and some taken down at an ecclesiastical hearing whose findings were discreetly filed away and never published. But if you can pick your way through it . . . '

With Murray at his elbow to point out the relevant paragraphs, Caspian pieced together the story behind Hexney's bonfire festival; and a very different story it was from that told by the Reverend Sebastian Wint.

There had indeed been an outbreak of plague in Hexney. But it was no subsequent fumigation that led to the great fire and the near-destruction of the village. The origins of the trouble dated further back than the most devout and most devilish participants realized.

After the Restoration of Charles II, official policy was the persecution of Dissent — including Roman Catholicism. 'While all the time, of course,' Murray observed, 'Charles himself leaned towards Rome. He'd married a Catholic, and later signed a secret treaty promising to restore Catholicism to England.' Priests did not find it too complicated to slip into England and establish discreet local congregations. Three such recusants made their way to Hexney, set on the junction of pilgrim routes to the old shrines of Walsingham, Bury St Edmunds, Ely and Croyland. But long before these paths had become pilgrims' ways they had served other travellers, other beliefs. The newly arrived priests had to minister to the faithful in an atmosphere pulsating with ancient intuitions and black, heretical blood music. They struggled to coax the villagers away from their sin; but being here only on sufferance could not be too open in their denunciations.

'And one of them' — Murray turned

over a page — 'brought the plague with him.'

When it spread through the village, the three priests warned pedlars and other wayfarers off the Hexney approaches and exhorted the villagers to stay within their walls until the scourge had passed. It must not spread over the entire region.

After a succession of horrible deaths and the burial of corpse after corpse in the fen, the inhabitants turned on these strangers in their midst. Ostensibly the spark that lit the kindling was anger over the fact that the plague-stricken priest still clung to life while so many of their own folk died. Picking his way through old print and inserted pages of yellowed calligraphy, Caspian could still sense the upsurge of old furies. Remembering Hexney all too well, he could imagine the pagan spells that would have been conjured. Some who had suffered persecution became, themselves, persecutors. There was the testimony of one settler who had sought refuge in England from Belgium, where his parents had suffered under the witch-hunt inquisitors. Now, he raged, the accursed Papists were plotting to seize power in England also and resume their torments here: and had also brought foul disease with them.

It was easy, even from this distance across the centuries, to picture the three priests as ready scapegoats whose sacrifice would appease older gods.

The patchy accounts of what took place added up to a hideous parody of a witchcraft trial in reverse. Two of the priests, one of them the sick man, were put through tortures such as those inflicted on witches and heretics throughout Europe. 'And the Great Shadow', read one torn scrap of paper folded into the book, 'thickened in the sky and rejoiced that in Her name the scales should be set to rights.' The third man escaped capture for a day or two, being hidden by a young woman to whom he had been giving instruction. Then she discovered that she too had contracted the plague and blamed him for it, and led him out into the clutches of his pursuers, denouncing him as a preacher of false doctrines to her.

He provided the culmination of the orgy of death.

'You are a blasphemer against the true gods and you bring pestilence into our land. Will you confess it freely?'

'I confess only to being God's faithful servant.'

His fingers were crushed under the blacksmith's hammer so that blood spurted from his nails. Still he admitted no fault. He was stripped, his hands were bound behind his back, and he was hoisted to swing from a gibbet in the marketplace with weights lashed to his feet. Then the rope was allowed to run free so that he smashed to the ground. Seven times he was hauled up and dropped, each time with heavier weights added. And each time he was asked: 'You brought lies and pestilence to this place; will you admit it and take them away with you?'

'I have a pure conscience in this matter.'

He was hoisted again, and his ankles lashed to the upright of the gibbet. Then flails were brought, and his legs beaten ceaselessly until bones and flesh were so torn that blood and marrow spouted forth.

'Take the guilt upon you.'

'I will pray for you and I will carry as much of the world's guilt as God gives me the strength to do. But I will not admit to the evil you impute.'

Thereupon he had no power to say any more, but hung there ragged and broken while the girl who had sheltered him and then betrayed him was scourged in the pillory until she, too, had no words left. But the men and girls of the village had words: songs, and jubilation, and dancing around the fire they had built. When the flames were raging as madly as the dancing, the gibbet was chopped through and the priest was borne face down on to the waiting pyre.

'And the Great Shadow was over the whole village and Her face was radiant out of the Shadow and Her promises were mighty and everlasting, and the people worshipped and feasted and danced and joined one to another.'

It was the burning of the priest that got out of hand. Blazing brands were scattered as the gibbet and its burden crashed into the pyre. Flames leaped at the houses around the square. Drunk on their own lusts, the villagers lost all control. Some perished; a few came to their senses in time and escaped to the fens. Some drowned, some were slaughtered: the scattered hamlets of the surrounding countryside wanted no plague-carriers wandering amongst them. At last a few survivors returned and began to rebuild.

Investigators who came in due course, drawn by rumours of what had seethed up in Hexney, were appalled by the relics they found and the stories they extracted piecemeal from a few surly witnesses. The matter was recorded but hushed up: a less grisly version of events was allowed to circulate for the benefit of the community and of posterity.

'It has always been an interesting debating point,' said Professor Murray, 'whether in any specific situation evil is done because destructive forces have been building up in men and have to be released in wickedness; or whether the evil is imposed upon them by . . . something outside mankind.'

'Or,' suggested Caspian, 'the man-made conditions are ripe for evil, and your demon from outside uses the situation as a catalyst for further and greater evil.'

'I hadn't thought you'd be one to postulate an actual Devil.'

'Purely a hypothesis. A debating point, as you said.'

'Ah,' said the professor keenly. 'Was it, now?'

They both felt the need for fresh air again, and went round to the terrace.

'There are still stories of odd goings-on in Hexney at certain times of year,' said Murray. 'And of occasional disappearances. One never knows how much credence to put in such tales. People do disappear at quite a rate in the fens, at the best of times: drowned, sucked into a marsh, or simply wandering off to the coast, going to sea.'

'Or to seek a better life in a city?'

'City life's not for many of them.'

Murray looked out across the parkland, reassuring in the discipline of its landscaping. 'Even in this day and age,' he said, 'I'd be none too happy to let anyone I was fond of venture too close to that place during one of its local anniversaries.'

Caspian nodded heartfelt agreement. He was glad Bronwen was not there for tomorrow night's bonfire; glad that, although they had mentioned it, in the end they had made no plans to return.

Then, without warning, he heard her cry out. Across fen and marshland the gap between them closed, and she made a howl of fear in his mind.

My dearest, if you were with me . . . to carry me away before . . . before . . .

Impossible. She was in Wales, she could not be anywhere else; and he could not hear her over so many miles. A coincidence, he told himself desperately. We've just been talking about Hexney, naturally I thought of Bronwen, I'm creating her voice in my own imagination.

I have been chosen, they're calling me, they'll use me. I'm frightened frightened.

'Ach, gentlemen, there you are.' The Prince of Wales strode along the terrace, ebullient and clearly in a mood to propose some fresh diversion. Caspian's expression brought him to a halt. 'My dear Count Caspar, something wrong? You look as if you'd just seen one of your own remarkable ghosts.'

★ ★ ★

A trap stood waiting at Hexney Halt. Nobody but Bronwen alighted from the train, but there were three or four travellers waiting to board it. She recognized Mr. and Mrs. Fortrey, dressed in their best and with a couple of cases and hatboxes. It was an odd time of year for them to be going on holiday.

Fortrey caught her eye and grinned evasively.

'Your inn's still open for guests, Mr. Fortrey? I didn't have time to notify you I was coming, but — '

'Oh, that's all right, miss. Your room's ready.'

'It could hardly be that.' She wondered

why she should trouble to demand logic in this, a situation beyond reason. 'I didn't notify you,' she persisted.

'Don't you worry 'bout that.'

He cast a furtive glance across the fen towards the village, then helped his wife into the compartment. The train puffed out as Bronwen approached the driver of the trap. He nodded without surprise, almost with affability.

They trotted along the causeway and up the slope of Hexney.

Leah Morritt was waiting to greet her on the step of The Griffin. 'Your room's ready, Miss Powys.' She grinned.

'I didn't notify you I was coming.' She said it again automatically, knowing it had no relevance.

The grin remained on Leah's moist, pudgy lips. 'Didn't need to, miss, did you? We knew you'd be back in time.'

She was given the same room. And it was ready for her, with fresh water in the carafe and hot water in the large jug. Clean towels had been hung on the bedrail. She began to unpack, and came across the stone where she had put it, tidily back in its silken pocket. The window was closed against the November cold. She flung it open and threw the stone out, hearing it crack against a cobble, seeing it ricochet away. But of course it was too late to discard it now. It had done its job: she had been brought where she was meant to be.

Bronwen went downstairs. There was no movement in the hall, or in the bar. She went out into the square and felt the bite of the winter mist on her cheeks. Here, out of doors, all was equally still.

She turned towards the gateway, and even before she reached it she saw the track that had been stamped up the lane, just approaching the edge of the market-place. Two footprints had come far enough to gouge out some cobbles, forcing them to one side and grinding two deep treads into the earth.

She stood in the arch of the gateway and looked out.

There was no sign of the houses from which women had looked out and brought her to a standstill. The railway halt ought to be visible from here; but it was not. It was not just a matter of braving the chill of the archway and striding off into the outside world. There was no outside world. No discernible landscape, no house or dyke or railway line. All Bronwen could see was a grey infinity, spreading wider than the fens had ever spread, plunging on down a hazy slope, which tilted more and more precipitously towards the abyss that waited beyond the rim of the world.

PART III

The Hub

1

On the green a heap of brushwood and lumber grew steadily around a tall central stake. Each villager, silently crossing and re-crossing the square, added a ritual mite: a broken branch, a handful of twigs, a splintered paling from some decrepit fence. The carpenter brought a sackful of shavings and splinters and clipped it on the pile. Five minutes later he returned with some newly planed timbers and began to erect a gibbet, dangerously close to the pyre.

There was a new hinge on the pillory, and Mrs. Morritt was polishing the blackened woodwork until it took on the shine of her grate.

Those moving in and out of the square did so in wordless reverie, content with the day and their small contributions to it. They were doing what had to be done with a minimum of fuss, conserving their energies for what was to come.

It was the early afternoon of Wednesday the fourth of November.

On her way back to Hexney, as on her way from it, Bronwen had stayed overnight in Shrewsbury in order to arrive at a reasonable hour of the day. She had lunched on the train from a small picnic basket only to find on arrival that a solitary place had been laid for her in the dining room of The Griffin.

'But how could you know I was coming?' Half a dozen times she phrased the question one way and another to Leah and the taciturn couple looking after the inn, receiving in answer only a sly smile or a hitch of the shoulder.

The few men in the taproom were impenetrably silent. Either they had run out of words or felt no further need of them. When Bronwen passed the open door to go out they turned to look at her, nodded, and returned to contemplation of the gleaming counter and tankards.

She noticed something that had not immediately caught her attention when she reached the inn. Shutters had been bolted across several windows in the square. She ventured down the lane towards the woodsheds between cottages boarded up with planks and even a couple of old barn doors. Nobody was working in the sheds, and although they were only a few yards away from the gap in the wall they seemed blurred and remote, like shapes in a badly exposed plate. Bronwen took a step through the wall; and was brought to a standstill by fierce cold, choking her, worrying her as a savage animal might. She struggled free and lurched backwards into the doubtful security of the village.

Nobody in the sheds, and nobody working out on the dykes. All the men were at home in Hexney: all those who had not boarded up their homes and taken their families away. Foreigners, she thought: those who were not truly Hexney folk of long descent, all gone, out of the way until it was over. Even the Fortreys. They had seemed very much a part of the place; but she remembered the Fortrey gravestones set apart, and what the Reverend Sebastian Wint had said about the few survivors of immigrant families. And now she remembered the face of one of the others on Hexney Halt with the Fortreys, waiting for the train. The wife, she was sure, of that odd young man called Jephson. Will Jephson, that was it. He must have married outside the village, and his wife knew when it was best for her not to be here.

Yet if they had left the village what was a stranger like herself, Bronwen Powys, doing here: for what had she been recalled?

She turned her steps towards the church in the hope of coaxing some sort of explanation from the rector. Inside, she came to a standstill as abrupt as when the outer cold had clawed at her.

Everything was veiled. A black shroud covered the altar, the font was a shapeless hump beneath black cloth, and fine black mesh obscured the statue of St Etheldreda and texts on the few family monuments. At an earlier time of year she might have supposed herself in a church whose incumbent took Lenten observances to a fanatical extreme.

There was only one splash of colour on

the walls. The curtain had been drawn half back from the painted Doom to expose those fleshy sinners who had been chosen for hell-fire.

Bronwen went out through the porch again. A figure as black as those within was coming up the lane from the rectory. Beside the churchyard wall two women dipped him a frightened curtsy. Bronwen raised her hand to attract his attention, and he came through the gate and up the path. But he was not the plump Mr. Wint. This man was younger and thinner, walking with his head lowered in a disturbingly guileful aura of pietism. Reaching Bronwen, he raised his eyes. In his emaciated, ageless features they gleamed a deep bronze yellow.

* * *

Hannah Morritt had been polishing the seamed woodwork of the pillory for more than an hour but felt no inclination to stop. She heard the hammering of nails into the gibbet, and the occasional crunch as somebody tossed more fuel against the stake; and she was soothed.

Gregory crossed the green, looking back at his mother as she polished, keeping his distance. He had nothing to say. Nor had she. The time for talking was past, and he knew it.

What he didn't know was that he was bespoken. Tomorrow night he would be hers.

Tomorrow night, when what we most dearly wish shall be granted. I know what *he* wants and what he thinks he'll be granted. Fool. Still wants that slut and still thinks he may take her back. But she's somebody else's tomorrow night. And Gregory's mine.

Mrs. Morritt was no longer angry. She was quite calm in her hatred and her knowledge of what must be. The foreknowledge was a satisfying accompaniment to the steady rubbing of her hand and cloth along the pillory as she polished and polished, putting all her weight behind it until it was a wonder the timber itself wasn't impregnated with her joy.

Gregory paused with his back to her.

That head. His father's ugly hands, and

that great ugly head. How it had torn her when she was delivered of him. And that muddy skin — how she had always loathed the feel of it when she bathed and nursed and dressed him, and cleared up his foul messes. He ought never to have been born. She had always been a good mother and worked hard to love him and to be forgiving even when no love was returned. Hating him was a private thing that she talked about only to herself, and only when things got too dreadful to be endured. But tomorrow she could stop pretending. She had waited so long. Now there would be an end to lying: a time when desire would prevail over falsehood. Right from the moment when the first footstep appeared from the fen she had prayed her claim. Whatever Gregory hoped for himself, he was too late. Her claim would win.

He glanced back as if he had heard her and wanted to protest.

Too late.

★   ★   ★

'Mr. Wint isn't about?'

'Mr. Wint is taking a week's well-earned rest.' The level voice gave no indication of whether the man was young or old. 'I have the privilege of serving in his place.'

Bronwen thought of the shuttered houses; of the Fortreys and Will Jephson's wife and those others who had fled; and of the cowardice of the rector also, deserting his flock; finding it best, in his own words, not to meddle.

'An inclement season,' she said, 'for a holiday.'

'A rest rather than a holiday. It has been known before.' He smiled with thin lips but not with those searing eyes. 'There's no reason to be alarmed for the Reverend Wint, I assure you.'

'You . . . your own parish . . . ?'

'I have no regular living. I wait to be called upon. But — ' the smile widened to exhibit teeth as yellow as his eyes — 'I never lack an occupation.'

She forced herself to look away, back at the church. 'The veiling in there — it's an odd time of year, isn't it? Holding a service must be difficult.'

'We shall practise our devotions out of doors this week.'

'Is that some new observance — something local?'

'On the contrary. Old and universal. What is new is the shutting away of congregations into solemn buildings. Ashamed — with every reason, I agree — of their petty little rituals and their denial of what their blood tells them.' Somehow she did not dare to meet his gaze again. 'The Ancient Worship,' he said sonorously, 'has always taken place under sun and moon and sky and the powers of the air. As you will see.'

Now she might have asked her question. But he left her without another word and went back the way he had come.

Bronwen waited until he was out of sight, then ventured down the lane to the priory, clicking her heels as noisily as possible on the cobbles. She refused to be lulled into this all-pervading trance that was settling on the village.

But wondered how long she would be able to refuse.

She had half expected the priory to be clouded by the same grey, distancing veil as the woodsheds. But the stony ruins were stark and clear, just as she remembered them. She tried a foot on the grass, then took a few steps.

The cold did not strike.

She walked down the slope. Beyond the jagged teeth of columns and crumbling walls was the vista she had glimpsed through the gateway and past the sheds — a descent into far oblivion. The priory, though outside the village wall, was nevertheless within some psychic perimeter. Warily she tried to establish the line of the barrier; for a barrier there must be.

Its chill struck her close to the outer wall, where the anchorite's cell jutted out from the ruins. She stepped back, and tripped on loose rubble. As she groped for the rough surface of the wall to steady herself, a small avalanche of stones trickled over her foot and into a gully.

They revealed a gap in one side of the cell.

Bronwen stooped to look in. The daylight over her shoulder was thin and unhelpful. To get a reasonable view of the interior she would have to squeeze in and let her eyes adjust to the shadows and broken shards of such light as there was. She stepped carefully down, testing the stones underfoot to make sure that she did not turn her ankle.

When she slipped, it was not on stone but something different, which rattled and shifted so that she had to clutch at the inner wall.

Pale light fell on a cache of bones.

The pitiful remains of some anchorite, she thought, walled up here to die many centuries ago. Yet it was strange that the iconoclasts who destroyed the abbeys of England should not have dispersed these bones rather than leave them as a possible focus of secret pilgrimage and veneration.

As she grew used to the vague twilight, she saw dark streaks down some of them. When she prodded one closer to the gap in the wall she saw that it had been charred. And surely there were the crumpled skeletons of more than one person immured here? Plague victims — or victims of that fumigation which, according to Wint, had got out of hand?

She forced herself to go down on her knees and examine the jumble of remains more closely. There were other burnt and blackened fragments: a length of leather belt, the metal eyeholes of a pair of boots — and, on one skeletal finger, a cheap ring which had buckled but not melted. As she touched it, it slid along the bone. There was an inscription inside: just initials and a date. The date was 1825.

These charred bones belonged not to the devout past of the priory nor to the plague-stricken past of the village, but to this century.

2

I am frightened but they shall not see it. Caspian, my love, if you were here with me, taking my hand, giving me courage . . . But no, that's cowardice. I have no right to call him.

I am not frightened. I refuse to be frightened. They shan't use me, they shan't prevent my walking out of this detestable place when I choose. Tawdry little superstitions, crude clod-hopping appetites — how can they scare me if I refuse to be scared?

And if I were to call out again, he's too far away to hear.

Bronwen walked back to the inn, ashamed of the impulsive plea for help she had silently screamed into the ether on her journey to Hexney and of the mounting urge to cry out again before they silenced her. She must resist. She could not grasp the full meaning of what had brought her here, but whatever it was she would defeat it on her own.

Before they use me.

Carrie Lavater crossed the end of the lane and stood transfixed.

'Oh, miss. You're back.'

'Yes,' said Bronwen, 'I'm back. Wasn't that what you intended?'

'Miss, I'm sorry. I didn't want to do it.'

'But you did it.'

'I'm sorry. Honestly I am, miss. But I couldn't bear to call him — not my Billy.'

'So you called me instead,' said Bronwen acidly

The girl blinked. Whatever she meant to say was slipping through her grasp. With a puzzled little shake of the head she managed:

'No that's not it at all. I thought you knew. I passed it on to you — the duty — for you to do the calling.'

Then it was as if she had gently died on her feet. Unseen fingers drew a mask over her eyes, as fingers might draw down a dead woman's eyelids. She turned and went on her way.

Dusk was settling over the rooftops, darkening the tiles and etching deeper shadows into alleyways. The chimney pots of empty houses gave out no smoke.

Life was suspended. Hexney waited, un-breathing.

The taproom door was still open. The interior was still real, still three-dimensional. Yet the figures in it could have been the photographs. A sepia interior, with still life. If she had walked in and nudged one and asked him to move six inches to the left in order to balance the composition, would he have mechanically obeyed? With no will of their own, whose orders would they accept?

Leah crossed the hall and passed her in an unnaturally straight line.

Bronwen said: 'I want to ask you . . . '

But Leah did not falter. She was gone.

The man running the inn during Fortrey's absence came out by the flap of the bureau.

Bronwen tried again, more forcefully. 'Tomorrow evening. Bonfire Night. Just what is it going to be? How do things usually go?'

Bonfire, she thought, and thought of its derivation: a bone-fire.

He said: 'What time would you be

wanting to eat this evening, miss?'

'I asked you — '

'Just wondered what time'd suit you best. Make the most of it, like. Won't be much time, mebbe, tomorrow night.'

She started past him into the dining room. Two places had been laid at one table. The others were, so far as she could make out, bare.

'Don't rightly know, do we, what time to expect him?'

They were all sinking deeper into their trance. They spoke what they had in them to say, ignoring or deflecting questions, which to them did not belong in the same conversation.

From her bedroom window, and from the dining room window as she ate without tasting, she saw the sprawling dark pyramid of the faggots and the silhouette of the gibbet against a turbulent sky. But though the clouds raced, everything within the village was still.

Bonfire and gibbet, waiting for the sacrifice.

A sacrifice. The thought of it had been in the air ever since she arrived. It was in all their thoughts: sitting mutely at home or standing at their accustomed places in the taproom, preparing, waiting.

She was to be the sacrifice. They would not offer up one of their own kind. They had chosen her and lured her back.

For you to do the calling: that was what Carrie Lavater had said.

I shall call nobody.

Sickeningly she thought of Caspian. But the call had been suppressed; and over such distances he would not have heard her or understood.

Eating, she stared at the cutlery opposite, and the folded napkin, waiting.

No. Fervently she denied it. I haven't tried to bring him to Hexney. They shan't use me or frighten me, and they'll not see Alexander Caspian in this place again.

Perhaps even now he had written to her in Wales and was wondering why her answer took so long to come.

In her room she sat late beside the fire. Peat in the grate burned languidly, with an occasional shift and splutter and an occasional spark from the few lumps of wood that had been added. Surprising that they could be spared from the bonfire.

She drew the curtains to banish the dark shape outside and at last climbed into bed. Often, on return from London or some other city, she had lain in bed at home by firelight and listened drowsily to dream rhythms lapping the outskirts of consciousness. In London one forever sensed the suffocating weight of other people's thoughts, clamorous by day and fretful by night, as relentlessly noisy as the unceasing rumble of traffic. In Caernarvon the clamour faded below a soothing music of waves and wind. Here in Hexney the night ought to have been even quieter. Instead, she felt the insistence of a single rasping idea, as powerful in sleep as it had been during the daylight hours. Yawning, she was in danger of sliding down into acceptance, into oneness with that thought. They all took it for granted that she could not fight free.

Should she force herself to stay awake by the window, watching the footprints, watching for what might come to tread the last few steps?

She could not force herself out of bed. She must wait, like the rest of them. There was nothing to be done now.

She slept.

Her dreams were of stars and triangles and strange configurations, which refused to fit into the pattern she knew was preordained. She struggled to count out loud, convinced that by doing so she could persuade the geometry of the puzzle to obey her. Her voice strained in her throat. Just to confuse her, someone was beating time, coming closer, destroying the rhythm.

She awoke to the sound of hoofs clattering across the square, and the panting of a hard-ridden horse. There was a pounding on the door below. After a pause it was repeated. The footsteps ... not merely marching but galloping right up to the door of The Griffin? That was nonsense.

Suddenly she knew, and was wide-awake. As bolts thumped back below, she went to the door of her room and opened it. Up the stairs came voices.

Leah first. 'Your room's ready, sir.'

And then the one she had known it must be. 'I was expected, then? Miss Powys made some arrangement with you?'

'Didn't have to. We knew.'

Bronwen, her dressing gown drawn about her, was on the landing as Caspian reached the top stair. He smiled.

'I made the best time I could.'

She shook her head, denying his presence here. 'What have I done?'

Leah came past Caspian and opened a door for him. She wore only a long, grubby shift, loose at the neck, and her hair was in a tangle over her shoulders.

'You've fetched him, dear, that's what you've done.' She recited it like a verse, which she was proud to have got off by rote. 'You was picked for it and you've done it just right.'

Caspian looked back at Bronwen from the doorway of his room. She felt the touch of his hand and heard his voice in her head, distinct from all others in Hexney.

Go back to your room, my love, and we'll talk.

You must go. Get away from here. I didn't want you to come, it was a moment of weakness. Go now.

I think it's too late for that.

I should have faced it alone. I'm ashamed.

You will not be ashamed, or afraid, he said firmly. *And you will not be alone.*

★ ★ ★

They were separate, in separate rooms in this alien place. But as she lay in encroaching darkness while the last ember faded in the grate, she felt him beside her. His mind reached out for hers, and she took it and drew it in. They lay with walls and a corridor and bedclothes and the slumbering menace of the Hexney night between them; yet with nothing between them. And he said:

Shall we marry?

We must talk first.

Talk is a sham. You and I have gone beyond such deceits.

This is not the time —

This is the time. We are in mortal peril. We die apart or, if we're strong enough, we live together.

She stared up into a future that might not last more than a few hours. His mind withdrew, leaving her to her own doubts and decisions. The loss left her empty. In sudden fear of losing him she called him back, and at once it was as if his breath were warm against her shoulder.

He asked: *Do you wish me to say that I love you?*

He was right. They had gone beyond sham and deceit. There was only one thing she could say. *I know that you love me. And you know that I love you.*

Then we shall marry?

Yes.

Understanding slowly suffused her, as slow and caressing as Caspian's gentle entry into her mind. They approached each other not in any conventional wedding ceremony but in a mystical marriage of mind and body. He had won the declaration from her and now was not hurrying her. For an hour they lay motionless while imperceptibly a hundred wisdoms and then a thousand welled up from the recesses of his memory and became hers. At the same time a current flowed from her own secret places, carrying gifts for him to accept or reject, until at last there would be a balance like the slow evening-out of water-levels in a lock, and the gates would stay open and there would be no separate knowledge, no you or I and nothing unshared, nothing held in reserve.

Lines beyond which there could be no trespassing.

Wasn't that what he had said in London?

They trespassed; and loved.

In that hour the name of Hokhmah became as familiar to her as if she had revered it all her life. And from the other side advanced Binah. She opened herself to the two principles, sought the shade of the two branches of the Tree of Life. With Caspian first at her side, then above her, embracing her, she was coaxed into the protracted sensuality of the Kabbalah's ritual union. Their minds as naked as their bodies, they explored each other without impatience, savouring the nuances of the *congressus subtilis.*

He and she were indivisible. Her sensations were his; his slowness and swiftness pulsed to the same rhythm as her own invitation and rejection; she gripped his thoughts and they became flesh, she flinched away from the stranger and craved the insistence of the lover. His exultation was an assault, but she too was the invader — the driver and the driven, the sword and the wound. She lay open and alone on the bed, but his mouth crushed hers and she carried his weight.

You are love and woman and will enfold. He is wisdom and man and must quench his heat in your cool waters, stir new life from your quiescent depths . . .

'No.' It was the first thing she had said aloud into the empty room.

She denied him. Denied her own subjugation, her eternal quiescence. Then she laughed, and called him a name she hadn't known before, and knew that they were indivisible. Her passion and his were indistinguishable.

The harmony Bronwen had sought was meaningless. Life was forever discord, the beauty of clash and dissolution, and then the coming together in a new, enriching dissonance.

I take you to be my ordained husband.

I take you to be my ordained wife.

They made free of each other, and were raised towards the high infinitude of the seven-fold *sephiroth,* in which all potency and all potentiality are one and un-wearying and indestructible.

And then they faltered.

She felt Caspian's body and soul shake within her. All that had been beautiful was blotted out by a black turmoil, a rain of cruelty dripping from the Tree of Life and sprouting poisonous growths, which grew at insane speed, groping out to choke the stem of creation.

Before Bronwen could call on Caspian to stay close and strengthen her, she was enveloped in a cloud writhing across and out of his mind. She stared into the heart of a darkness so vile that instinctively she tore herself away — from him, from the cloud, from what raged in its depths. Evil gave out an emanation so obscene that she cried aloud. A face gibbered up from the pit; not a face that had ever revealed itself on earth, save perhaps to some madman lost beyond all hope. There was a stench that was no smell but all senses run together into an ultimate putrescence. She tried to turn her head away, her body away, her consciousness away.

And she felt Caspian, despairing, bidding her farewell: setting her free before it was too late.

Too late.

She rebelled. Fear for him was greater than her own fear. She stared back at the maelstrom of evil and gripped his arms. He was trying to shut his mind, to spare her what snaked and reared and slavered in its deepest abyss, but she knew her way into his far reserves now and flowed back in, denying the terror and holding him to her and dragging him back from the monstrous cloud.

Until slowly the serpentine fumes began to disperse. Light shone through. Somewhere in the universe there was dawn. The white magical force of what she knew to be the loving Shekinah spread its radiance over their marriage beds.

They were drained and exhausted. It was a long time before she found it in her to speak.

You've accused others of fraud and

304

trickery. But you're a deceiver.

His mind stirred under hers.

Where did that abomination come from — how did you summon it?

She felt his protest, though there were no words for it. Then, as she accused him again, painfully the words began to come.

You have cheated, she goaded him.

He gave in.

She had shared the horror with him and knew that it put an end to all his protestations of there being a mechanistic, scientific explanation for all phenomena. It had been with him for a long time and doggedly he had kept it at bay, refusing to admit it was there: something so appalling that it had to be locked away at the back of his mind.

And yet you have condemned others, those who have sensed the other world and its mysteries, of charlatanry.

Most of them . . .

'What was it?' she demanded aloud into the bleak morning hours. 'When did it first lay hands on you?'

Reluctantly, hating her to feel and share his fear, he let the story leak through to her, reining it back when it threatened to break loose and become too vivid again.

At the end of one of his European tours, presenting his own illusions to spellbound audiences and learning other spells as he went, he found himself with some weeks to spare. He took the opportunity of returning to Prague, where he had once been a student; this time he wanted to study, with respectful scepticism, the tenets of the great Kabbalistic scholars, whose tradition had remained unbroken in the city for centuries. Already an avowed antagonist of spiritualists and their frauds and fandes, Caspian felt he might learn from the Kabbalists how less scrupulous mystics had contrived to mislead a less studious public.

And perhaps, Bronwen thought, there was a need in himself, which he had refused to avow.

He evaded the glance of her thought and went on.

Accepting the disciplines of his tutors, yet doubting them as he did so, he shut himself away, first for one day, then for two, then for three days in meditative trances. The first day he was merely irritated, blaming himself for the folly of coming here at all. His mind was not empty and receptive, but filled with contempt for his fellow human beings and for himself. Yet he was drawn back for the two days of fasting and contemplation in which he felt the intimations of a strange, elusive happiness, gone as soon as he tried to turn his full attention upon it; and touched the concept of the biune spirit of Manifested Being, but was not allowed to assimilate the full essence of it. He continued to fast and, after preparation and warnings by the adepts, entered on the three-day meditation. In this he learned what he had imparted to Bronwen: the splendour of the Tree of Life, the occult influences on all human philosophy and human behaviour of Kether the Crown, Hokhmah and Binah, Hod the giver of Eternity and Yesod the Absolute, and the harmonies within the immortal circle and its triad.

Until, beyond the light, he allowed himself to ask questions against which the adepts had warned him, and to doubt and despair in a fatigue of the soul which turned all tastes sour and all vision dark. In that black night of the soul he found himself on the edge of an abysm of utter evil, like a man in dream scrambling on a rock face with nothing but death below — a death so hideous that, without looking down, he knew what had driven saints to martyrdom and hermetic adepts to insanity. A million slavering mouths that made one mouth gaped for him. A face wider than hell formed out of the foulness of the pit. He knew it was there, but still did not look directly down; he clawed at the rock and somehow was running, fleeing back to the remote promise of light.

And have been fleeing ever since.

In spite of his attempts to shield her from the full dreadfulness of the pit and its palpitating floor of demons, he could not repress thin trickles of terror, which oozed through the interstices of his mind as blood and pus might ooze from a torturer's boot. The picture of the boot came to her with sickening vividness; and simultaneously she learned all that he had learned from Professor Murray at Sandringham.

There was so much she knew, now. All his materialism and analytical arrogance had been defensive. At the forefront of his civilized mind, even now, he desperately denied the experience in Prague. She felt him already trying to explain it away as he had so often explained it to himself: the result of unhealthy fasting and consequent hysteria.

That was why he had shown such implacable enmity towards mediums and soothsayers of every kind: to the possibly genuine ones even more than to the charlatans.

It's not that you disbelieve, she accused him, but that you dared not believe, and still do not dare.

He tried to blanket her with drowsiness.

They must rest; sleep; they would need all their strength tomorrow.

She caught at a moment of inattention and glimpsed a trail of footprints across his mind. No, there were two, one overlaid by the other and then somehow intertwined: one track in snow, one in brown earth.

Devon, she thought. He had been born in Devon. On what date? He could not withhold the answer, which she had already phrased for herself. On that night in February 1855 his mother had been forced to stay in Exmouth, visiting friends, because of a heavy snowstorm and a vicious cold snap. Feeling her labour pains earlier than anticipated, she was unable to set out for home because of the un-slackening snowfall. In the intense cold the River Exe itself was freezing over. So Alexander was born not at Littleham, as planned, but at Exmouth.

Born on the night when the devil's footsteps raced across the snow and ice.

And you have always been afraid that something . . . somebody . . . came for you.

He tried to shut her out.

And you're afraid it may come again. But why you?

If he knew, he could not tell her. She hardly dared to ask any more. Only in her own mind, with his grip on it sleepily relaxing, did she ask whether he was afraid that this was what they were doomed to meet tomorrow.

But there were two of them now. It could not separate them.

Weariness claimed her. It seemed that his arms were wrapped protectively around her; yet at the same time she was the enfolder, the protector.

★ ★ ★

A restless wind across the levels tortured itself into a gale. It gathered strength as it raged along the droveways and began to whip up the waters of the fen. A dyke burst. Shallow ripples chewed at the railway embankment and gradually encircled the foot of Hexney's hill; but did not reach the priory. The wind grew louder, shrieking up to the gateway; but not through it.

Sealed off from whatever irrelevant world might exist outside, Hexney dreamed its steady dream, stirred, and at last woke to the steely grey dawn of the fifth of November.

3

In the still centre of the whirlwind Caspian and Bronwen crossed the market-place arm in arm, a honeymoon couple who should have been murmuring fond jokes together. Anywhere else, eyebrows might have been raised at such a forward young woman leaning on a man's arm, so obviously speaking words of love even when her lips did not move. But Hexney was pre-occupied. The couple were of no consequence in themselves: not yet; only figures waiting, like the rest, for the appointed hour.

No wind breached the walls or blustered down from the sky. But greyness flooded up to the hill and covered the village like a transparent roof.

The footsteps had kicked up several more cobbles and trodden the green to within a yard of the pyre. Caspian had heard nothing in the night: they had been allowed to hear and see nothing.

He led Bronwen towards the gateway.

'Last time,' she said, 'together, we were able to . . . '

Together. In spite of what was building up all about them, they smiled. He touched her secretly, lovingly, and she gasped. 'Sir!'

'My love.'

Had they spoken aloud or not? It seemed no longer to matter. After last night, inner speech and the sounds of tongue and throat grew harder to differentiate, minute by minute.

Nobody else was listening. Nobody saw or sensed their quick flare of passion, the touch and protest and laughter. Nobody watched: they were all so secure in their trance.

Caspian gripped her arm, and his mind gripped hers.

'Now!'

They walked resolutely under the arch.

Cold was not just a cloudburst pouring itself stunningly on them, but a vicious blow, which knocked them backwards so that their feet slithered and strove for a grip on the cobbles. They paused for breath and tried again, willing themselves to see the hill and cottages outside, the fen and railway line and station.

As if the wind had been summoned up in reply, they were hurled back again.

'This time,' said Bronwen, 'it has grown too strong.'

'Only because we've persuaded ourselves to expect something of the kind. Or we've allowed the weight of the villagers' thinking to numb us. If we can only think ourselves into *disbelieving* . . . '

They tried the gateway again, insisting that as they had come in without difficulty they should leave without difficulty.

The icy barrier did not crack.

'We must learn to refuse,' said Caspian. 'Refuse to believe. We must. Whatever illusion they set before us or before themselves, we must reject it as what it is — illusion. Refuse to believe,' he repeated.

'Mobs have won many a day, whatever their victims believed or didn't believe.'

They picked their way between the footprints. The pentagram — they shared the thought — was sealed. The Dunstall boy had been drowned to complete one side, and now the footprints had tightened the entire knot. Bronwen found the marks so familiar now, from studying and photographing them with professional detachment on that first visit, as to be almost innocuous.

She said: 'That was why you came here, wasn't it? To see what they could tell you about that other trail — and about yourself?'

His mind confided in her. She shared his puzzlement, his guesses and rejections. Astrological conjunctions, then and now? He admitted that in moments of weakness he had dabbled with such a speculation. Then he snatched the confession back from her. Some line of descent through his mother from some earlier prey far back in Transylvania — alchemist, conjuror, perverted mystic? Something in the blood, which would always draw the predator? In Devon the occult trap had failed to close because, thanks to the snow, his mother had given birth not at home but in Exmouth.

Yet if there were such a beast of prey, an elemental, with such supernatural powers and such foresight, would it not have foreseen his mother's change of plan or at the very least detected it at the last moment?

'If the forces of evil got all their calculations right and foresaw every shift and subtlety,' said Bronwen, 'they would long ago have won. An infallible Devil would make a mockery of the whole philosophy of the cosmos.'

'And isn't it a mockery?' He stared impotently at the gateway. 'Talking!' he exploded. 'Here we are, left to our own devices, ambling about talking and theorizing as if . . . as if . . . '

Three girls walked demurely past The Griffin, all in starched cotton dresses which would have been more appropriate to a summer's afternoon than this November morning. One would have expected them, too, to be chattering and giggling together, or at the very least looking about them. But they looked neither to right nor left, and made no sound; and their gaze was fixed on some invisible something ahead.

'Until they're ready for us,' said Bronwen, 'what is there to do but talk?'

The carpenter leaned a short ladder against the gibbet and climbed up with a coil of rope over his shoulder. He secured it, and began to test the weight and pull of a bulging sack, prodding it to make it swing.

Leah Morritt leaned against the knocking-post at the entrance to the stable yard with her arms folded, two fingers curling in to rub the fur tippet between her breasts.

Will Jephson added a kettleful of hot water to the cold tin bath in the scullery, stripped, and began to wash with hard yellow soap. Cold as it was, he was content to take his time. There was no work to be done today, and no eating until nightfall: nothing to do but make ready. The cottage was quiet without Sarah singing and clattering from room to room, but there was hardly a ghost of her in his head. Even if that scene by the priory had been true, it no longer mattered. He had seen it because he wanted to see it, and it had freed him. The lies and nonsense had been cleared away, along with Sarah. He soaped himself and looked at the wall, and looked down at himself, and thought about Leah. Only it wasn't thought but sheer hunger. It had gnawed at him for a long time, could have eaten him away without him knowing it if he hadn't woken up. Tonight it would be satisfied.

Hannah Morritt tidied and dusted her sitting room, and polished her grate, and hummed the tune of an old hymn she had been teaching the children.

Two sloe-eyed children, crouched on the kerb drawing circles and grotesque faces in the dust, glanced up to see a stray cat squeezing itself between loosely-fitting slats of a fence. They stayed as they were, quite motionless. The cat licked one paw and turned along the lane. It must have been left behind by one of the departing families. The children made enticing, smacking noises with their lips, until the cat stopped, considered, and then came towards them. They made no move until it was in the gutter between them. Then one stabbed down with his right hand, got the cat by the neck, and carried it squawking indoors. The other followed. They knew it would be needed.

★ ★ ★

Bronwen said: 'Why have these footsteps taken so long to reach their destination, compared with those in Devon?'

'If we are to assume something otherworldly, outside our natural laws —'

'Isn't it about time we did?' she said wryly.

'For the sake of argument, then.' He was stubborn, fighting to the last. 'If we can envisage some cosmic cat's-cradle in which mankind is occasionally entwined — by accident, or as part of an astrological unity we're not yet capable of understanding — there's no reason why the time scale should always be the same. There must be fluxes and complexities far beyond our comprehension. Those other footsteps — in Devon, racing a hundred miles in a few hours, in other places and at other times leaving only a few prints or even just one mark, leaping away again into the unknown. Here at Hexney there has been a slow building up of forces, to enclose and cast a spell which utilizes all the latent rhythms of local ritual — the Gathering, the ancestral memory of ritual murder . . . and now the night of the bonfire.'

'And did we come here by accident, or by design?'

'Perhaps not our own design. But I don't think,' said Caspian, 'that it was anticipated we would marry.' *Or perhaps I was summoned, and you were an unexpected factor, which was then made use of. Perhaps you could have stayed clear of the completed occult knot if you hadn't been drawn in — forced in — by Carrie Lavater. At that juncture there were still alternatives, imponderables, possible adjustments.* 'Forced into it.' He came to a halt by the churchyard wall and looked over at the Fovargue and Fortrey graves. There, and there only, were the foreigners who remained. 'Of course. That's our only hope.'

She waited for his insight to pierce the confusion he had created, like a diver stirring up the inky mud of an unexpected crevice.

'Design,' he was saying. 'Mutual trance. Mutual acceptance. The rite can only be completed under prescribed conditions.'

'And if some jarring new element broke the pattern — '

'The Chesterfields found the presence of doubters at their séances distracting.' And on stage, Caspian himself had to be confident that every tiny piece fitted, every second counted. 'If we could introduce an eccentric factor,' he said, 'the equation wouldn't resolve.'

'We're sealed in. Nothing can throw it off now.'

'Our own disbelief — '

'Are we strong enough? And do we really disbelieve?'

The disbelief of others . . .

They looked quickly at each other, and he said: 'If only there were somebody left in the village. Someone not descended from that inbred race of Hexney lepers. Are we sure that all the others left?'

It was a flimsy, absurd hope, but it drove them down one lane and back up another, trying door latches and tapping on shutters as if to conjure up some last-ditch friend out of hiding.

Blank faces swam behind a few unshielded windows — the entranced faces of the possessed.

They passed Mrs. Morritt's house as she was cleaning the inside of a window-pane. Their minds, in tune, resounded to her undisguised intent.

Murder: the woman was planning the most barbarous murder.

She has been planning it for years, on the lower level of her consciousness. Too deep for it ever to be rooted out.

Bronwen said: 'But tonight — '

'Is the night when all restraints are lifted and the will is all.'

They escaped past the schoolhouse and into the square again, crossing it and exploring the lane which led out to the drove road. He walked to the left of the trail of footprints, she to the right. The wall on her side was blank; on his, there were three cottages. At the end, a plank hastily hammered across a window frame had sprung loose, creaking down on its remaining nail.

'Look at that,' said Caspian. 'Keep

looking at it. Could we bring somebody back from outside? We have received messages — can we transmit them? Concentrate ... and tell yourself it's worse than it looks. Make them see their house being wrecked ... pulled down, despoiled by the mob. If we could enrage just three or four of them into coming back, it might be enough.'

They linked minds in a creation of violence, saw wood torn down and glass splintering, flame licking up at thatch, and were smitten by what swam up out of the chaos: the other minds in Hexney, waiting, gleeful in contemplation of death and fire and destruction.

They wrenched themselves free.

Grant us our unbelief.

When they returned to the inn, Leah had taken up a fresh stance in the front doorway, hardly bothering to edge aside so that they might pass. Her placid face turned to appraise them. It was not her own pleasure but the pleasure of the entire village that curled her lips approvingly.

The words spoken to Caspian last night

went on ringing in Bromven's ears.

'What have I done?' she asked again, at the foot of the stairs. 'What did that girl mean about me being picked for it, and doing it just right?'

'I think I know. I think there's only one thing it can be.' He was some paces away from her, but she felt his hands lightly on her shoulders, and beneath the fold of her muslin fichu he was kissing her throat. *My beloved.* 'In all rituals — the sabbat, the Templar rites, Masonic rites, sacrificial ceremonies — there always has to be an introducer. A sponsor of the novice. Or presenter of the offering.'

'But all along I've thought . . . I've been so sure . . . *I* was to be the sacrifice.'

'You're the bringer and presenter of the sacrifice. I'm the one chosen. And who more reliable than you to call me when the time was near?'

My love, what have I done?

My wife . . . my dearest.

As the overcast sky deepened to twilight, tears choked in her throat and stung her eyes. She saw sparks and winking glow-worms through a blur: oil lamps were

324

being turned up and set in windows, candle flames shimmered, dots of light made an irregular frieze between the dark patches of shuttered houses.

Are we strong enough, just the two of us?

It was waiting to be fed. It would soon be upon them.

She knew what she must do.

What's that you're saying? Caspian, on the landing, came quickly after her.

Before he could reach her and before he could reach into her she bustled her thoughts into hiding, and refused to let him find them.

4

The heartbeat of the village quickened, steadied, and settled into an insistent drum tap. Flames of a smoky redness spurted and blossomed along the lanes. Groups of young men and girls raised torches above their heads and began to saunter towards the square. The saunter shaded into a march. Behind them trotted the smaller children of the village, some with tin drums and old saucepans, one with a tambourine, their arms like tiny pistons beating a ragged time until they, too, discovered a steady rhythm.

Their elders let them pass and then converged more slowly on the square. A few carried storm lanterns that they set on windowsills, along the churchyard wall, or in crannies in the stonework.

The tinny clank and rattle of drums and saucepans built up in volume.

It could have been any gawky, innocent country revel, thought Caspian: children's rapt faces, the thudding of their fingers and knuckles, young men and women waving their torches and grinning vacantly while older folk looked fondly on. But the tic of the drumming was too mesmeric, the children's fixed expressions too unnatural; the marchers' steps were those of well-drilled automata; and now the dour, seamed faces of the older folk were cracking open as they started a chant, all on one note, striking across the drumming and then taking up its insidious message. Once they had all reached the square they began to pace out its boundaries, lights swaying, voices keening, in a harsh processional hymn.

Caspian and Bronwen stood under the shelter of the lych-gate. No head turned in their direction as men, women, lads and girls and children marched past. But everyone knew they were there.

And would know where to find them and round them up if they broke away and ran?

Another figure appeared, solitary, by the churchyard wall. The priest, swathed in black from head to foot without even a hint of white, paid no immediate heed to the two standing apart from the procession. Their time would come. It had all been decreed.

He stepped out on to the green, raising his arms in what might have been a blessing. Then without a word he turned back, breaking the slowly circling procession again, and walked with his head bowed towards the lane and the slopes above the priory.

The circle broken, the children took the lead in following him, still staring solemnly ahead and beating time unceasingly.

Caspian made a move to bring up the rear, but Bronwen put a restraining hand on his arm.

Before them the square and the village lay deserted.

Somewhere there must be sanctuary.

Together they turned in through the lych-gate and hurried up the path. The church door was bolted. They followed the path round the building and down to a kissing-gate in the low wall above the priory, From here they had a view of torches blazing, swaying and smoking, and of white and red-tinged faces bobbing down the slope, disappearing briefly under an arch and reappearing near the site of the old altar.

Terribilis est locus iste.

The swish of feet through the grass died away. A stark black pillar beside the altar moved and became the priest, arms raised again. Reflection of torchlight was red and gold in his eyes.

There was a lull in the drumming. Against a far undertow of wind in another world his voice was jubilant and shrill.

'We are gathered here on this holy night to dedicate ourselves again to the holy spirit of this place.' Between each phrase he paused in a rhythm that took the place of the drumming and chanting which had driven the procession. 'We invoke the Great Mistress who was and is Artemis and Ashtoreth and Arianrod.' The torches were bright but unwavering, their smoke streaming up in fine straight threads. 'Sister and mistress and mother, whose feet crush the heavens and whose body encloses the universe.' The smoke trembled in a gentle, caressing breath. 'We ask to be scourged and exalted. We ask to be humbled and to rise up. We offer our pain and beg for your joy. The Dark Satellite is with you and with us, but will not stay. Draw down its power on us, we beseech thee, for we know we shall not see it again this century.' A faint moan round the entire assembly was lost among the jagged stones. 'Feed us that we may feed thee. Grant us the fury of joy that it may be returned to thee tenfold. In the names of the dead and the undead who were our forefathers and shall be with us again, who sang your praise that we may sing your praise, descend upon us, Mistress of Shadow and Substance.'

'Descend upon us,' came a murmuring echo.

The priest began to walk down the phantom floor of the nave, straining his voice higher to set off a wail of versicles and responses.

'Thine is the consummation.'

'Thine is the consummation.'

'Free us from shame.'

'Free us from shame.' The older ones mumbled, the young men and women carolled.

'To celebrate the Great Rite . . . '

'To celebrate the Great Rite . . . '

'And fill and fulfil thee . . . '

'And fill and fulfil thee.'

Pallid faces swirled into new patterns in the flame-scarred darkness.

'It's so crude,' said Bronwen in a whisper. 'Just a ludicrous travesty.'

'Would you expect an intelligent Devil to waste style and cunning corruption on a rabble of simpletons?'

'If they're such simpletons — '

'They are nonetheless dangerous. The cruder their minds, the more brutish their appetites.'

In the sombre grey ruins below, the priest reached the skeleton of the west door and cried: 'Who will commence the rite?'

Two naked figures, hot and gleaming in a night that ought to have been cold, stepped on to the grass beside the priory.

'Are you unclean?'

'I am,' said Leah Morritt gladly.

'Do you forswear the falsehoods of chastity?'

'I do.' Will Jephson roared it.

331

The priest raised eyes and hands in supplication to the dark roof thickening above the village.

'Accept the seed of these thy children.'

Torches dipped to cast a steam of infernal redness on what was once green. The young girls began to laugh a repetitive, rippling laugh, light and feminine and intoxicating, rippling lightly even when it had become a snarl.

On that spot where he had created the thrusting shadows in his mind, Will Jephson abandoned himself to the reality he had lusted for. Leah spread her body, flaunting it under the greedy light. He sprang across the grass and she rose to meet him.

Bronwen looked away, scared of surrendering to the frenzy of it, of losing all sense of the distinction between this and what she had known in the ecstatic night. Was there any distinction? Who was she to suppose, to resist, to . . . Caspian caught the revulsion of her thought, and she felt him move closer. It was as if he were entering her again, gently, subtly taking possession and reassuring her.

Abruptly she rejected him, jolted by his hurt as she escaped.

But he had come too dangerously close to the thought she must shield from him.

The metallic drumming which had started again was working up to a fever pitch. As the procession reformed it moved not into a march but a dance. Faster and more jubilant, it swung round the two bodies still locked shudderingly together on the ground, and set off up the slope.

'We mustn't be there when they get back,' said Bronwen. 'We must go — quickly.'

He seized her, not merely with his mind but physically, gripping her arms above the elbow. 'You're hiding something.'

'We agreed on some reservations.'

'Not at a time like this. Not when we need all our — '

'Come along,' she said, 'before it's too late.'

She hurried him across the churchyard and the end of the lane, up which came a surge of drumming and raucous singing. The drumming followed them down the next lane, seeming to beat within the timbers of every house. The whole village throbbed with the pulse.

There was no escape.

But she took him round the back of the Jephsons' house, and tried the scullery door, and found it open.

'But why here?' he demanded.

'Will Jephson won't be coming back tonight. And his wife's away.'

'They'll not rest until they've rooted us out.'

'The cellar — '

'How do you know there's a cellar?'

The picture of its muddy, clogged grille in the front wall, three inches up from the ground, was clear in her mind. It was at once clear to Caspian; and so was what lay behind it.

'No!' He had taken her off guard. 'You're not going to leave me skulking here and — '

'I brought you here. It should never have happened.'

'You're not going out there alone.'

'Please. Don't you see, if we're separated — if they do catch me, they don't want me. Not for myself. And if I refuse to speak — '

Can you think what they'll do to you?

She dragged him on into the echoing, stone-flagged kitchen. In the darkness he tripped, and she blundered against a table.

'Hush!'

They heard a rustling and scurrying. Their absence must already have been noticed — perhaps from the moment they began to run — and the rats were after them, sniffing and scuttling and squeaking on the scent: the pitter-patter and chattering and squeaking of children.

The cellar. If we separate, if you lie there till it's over . . . it has to end . . .

'While they tear you to pieces?' he said furiously.

A little girl's voice piped up from the far end of the lane. 'I can hear them, there they are, somewhere down there.'

Feet scurried eagerly. And all the time the beat of the music lulled and numbed.

Bronwen dragged her feet out of the kitchen, trying to avoid another collision, and into the narrow passage by the parlour. She could just make out the outline of a wooden door under the stairs. She groped for the latch.

'Who are you? What are you doing here?'

Sarah Jephson stood in the parlour doorway, light from the street window pale about her head.

Bronwen said helplessly: 'But you left. I saw you on the platform.'

'I changed my mind. I came back.'

'But it's closed. You — '

'Maybe the likes of you can't get out.' The girl was very quiet, filled with a quiet, pent-up determination. 'But there's no stopping someone coming back, if they're so minded.'

There was a rapping and scratching at the front door.

'I can hear summun, in there.'

The three of them remained frozen. Then Sarah's head turned slowly, as if she were beginning to listen more attentively to the thudding rhythm. Bronwen reached out to touch her, perhaps to pull her back — she didn't know, the gesture was instinctive. Abruptly Sarah went to the door and opened it. A little boy holding a lantern raised it above his head, and the five or six children around him raised their eyes to Sarah so that they shone, and their teeth shone in the yellowish glow.

'Missis . . . '

'In there.' Sarah stood aside, looking out over their heads, straining towards the rhythm, not looking back at Bronwen and Caspian. 'There,' she said dreamily.

The children swarmed in. They filled the cramped space, leaping and squeaking about their prey, and somehow there must have been more of them: they had the strength to bite and snap and drive Bronwen and Caspian into the lane and on towards the square, teeth chattering with glee.

Sarah closed her front door behind her and followed, gently swaying to the rhythm.

The marchers and dancers spread out around the square and then closed in upon the green, separating into a number of circles, like petals around the central pile of faggots, with the stalk of the gibbet jabbing up to one side.

A cockerel crowed and then screeched

once. There was a flurry in the dust; and then he was held up, his throat cut. The man from The Griffin bent over the group and handed a cup to the young man with the knife.

Gregory Morritt sagged with his head and arms through the pillory. A woman walked from a house on the corner of the square and, almost casually, tossed the contents of a chamber pot in his face.

Children shrieked with joy.

Then they turned their attention inwards, into their own pre-occupied circle. Two squawking cats were tossed at each other. They scuffled for a second. then turned to flee. The children leaned forward, each holding a blazing torch, and lowered the flames to enclose the animals in a ring of fire. The cats howled, turned in upon each other, and then made another bid for freedom. Flame jabbed at them. Fur singed.

Great Mistress, Great Mother of Sea and Earth and Under-Earth, come down and give birth.

The sky was a thousand shades of blackness, a whirlpool in which shapes formed and failed, looped and were lost in a swirl of tendrils, and then began to coagulate again.

Constable Rylot gazed up at the gibbet. He hadn't seen a good open-air hanging since he was a little lad. Hadn't seen a good hanging at all, come to that: it had never been part of his job.

One group of children kept up a steady drumming.

The priest led Mrs. Morritt reverently towards the pillory.

Caspian and Bronwen were jostled into the square as light was touched to the bonfire.

I will not believe. We will not believe.

From crackling branches, smoke rose to interweave with the turmoil of the sky. Flame licked suddenly forth.

Help our unbelief.

Two men, one of them the Hexney butcher, released Gregory Morritt from the pillory; but only for a moment. Holding him secure, they twisted him round and pushed his head backwards through its slot, and then bent his arms back until they threatened to break, pinned in place so that his weight hung towards the mounting fire.

The girls were dancing again.

Shaking off the children clutching his knees and goading him towards the green, Caspian sprang forward. He reached the narrow platform of the pillory and knocked the butcher to the ground. The other man braced himself against the woodwork and struck out. Caspian, timing it as he had timed many such an intended somersault, caught him by the wrist and tossed him back on to the cobbles.

The butcher picked himself up and lumbered back. Three other men detached themselves, as if at a signal, from a silent group near the fire, and threw themselves on Caspian. He disposed of two in a quick feint, but they came back, and the butcher was there, and he was brought to a standstill.

The priest nodded, and said to Mrs. Morritt: 'Now he is yours.'

She went to her son and began, almost lovingly, to undress him as far as she could. His coat and shirt were pulled open, and she carefully unlaced his boots

340

and pulled them off, dragged his trousers away from him, and stood back.

'Butcher,' said the priest gently.

The butcher moved away from Caspian and picked up a knife from the grass.

The girls' dancing slowed; their eyes turned greedily towards Gregory hanging half naked in the fierce firelight.

Just once Hannah Morritt hesitated, glancing back at the church as if some chord of memory had been faintly plucked. Then the priest moved closer, his head bending towards hers. She nodded. As the butcher advanced with his knife, she said clearly:

'No . . . let me do it.'

Caspian tried to fight free, but was held. Bronwen tried to turn away, sickened, but was hemmed in by a little ring of upturned, shining infant faces.

The body hanging from the pillory jerked convulsively, and moaned. As Mrs. Morritt tossed something into the fire, something which hissed and spat and sizzled, the butcher shook his head in pained but tolerant disapproval: not a very neat job. He stepped forward to guide her hand for the drawing.

Gregory's voice was lost in the humming and rippling laughter of the girls.

When his mother stepped aside, his entrails were the curling echo of the snakes which writhed in the sky, but a fiery red as they dropped towards the fire and began to roast.

Joshua Serpell sat slumped over the bar in the taproom of The Griffin. He had drunk too much, and ached, and felt like throwing his guts up. But there was nothing else to do, this night. He had nothing to offer: not enough hatred left, just aches and pains and an awful weariness with the world. He sat where he was, elbows and head on the wooden counter, adding just the tiniest loathing for life to the offering that reeked up from Hexney.

Around the green the reservoir of their hates and desires gave sustenance to the flame. Like a peat fire starting of its own accord beneath the fen and seething slowly to the surface, it set the earth smouldering until the darkness between heaven and earth was filled with smoke.

The cloud took on shape and substance as it began to feed.

The priest approached Caspian and bowed. 'Sir.'

'Don't taunt me.'

'I do not taunt.' His eyes were implacable but his tone was hushed and respectful. 'You have been of too much importance to be mocked. Too much loved and sought after. And now you have been brought to us.'

He held out his right hand, and the children around Bronwen prodded and bustled her across the last stretch of cobbles.

'You'll set us free,' said Caspian fiercely.

'Yes. From earthly bonds.'

Together we must reject what he wills us to see.

Together they glanced upwards. Great lips plopped and parted, and a dark saliva dripped on the village. They were staring dizzily upwards into the mouth of the abyss, reeling towards it to fall in or be gulped in.

We do not believe. We refuse to see.

Did the outline fade, writhe itself into a new shape, momentarily lose authority?

They denied its existence. But it was growing stronger, swelling out, expanding down from the sky, to meet something that was forming itself out of the earth. Out of the earth and water and the mud of their wedlock. Something primeval laboriously hauling itself out of primeval swamp, setting feet that were not yet feet into the path out of the droveway and into the village, squelching and splashing as it tried to rear up in its tracks.

The priest said to Bronwen: 'Take this man's hand, and lead him towards the fire.'

'No.'

'As it was ordained — '

'She will not lead,' said Caspian, 'and I will not be led.'

The men holding him turned him to face the fire, so that his face was scorched and his eyes dried and prickled in the heat

The priest said: 'It will be nobler if you go with the ritual rather than against it.'

'Nobler? For us — or for you?'

'Torment,' said the respectful voice, 'can be brief or eternal. The choice is yours.'

★　★　★

At Hexney Halt the floodwaters had risen to within fifteen inches of the railway line. There had been no warning of this back at Withersey, and for more than an hour the driver had waited here on the embankment, trying to make up his mind whether to press on or not.

'You all right, missis? You reckon you'll be safe there?'

'Won't come no higher. Not now.'

Mrs. Dunstall had been leaning on her fence since dusk, a fowler's oilskin over her shoulders and a shawl about her head, hardly taking her eyes off the strange spurts of light and smoke above the walls of Hexney. She was indifferent to the train and its driver, indifferent to whether they stayed, went on, or went back.

Passengers who had descended from the train huddled into the weatherboard and brick shelter. Like Mrs. Dunstall, they stared at the dark hummock of the village, breathing red fumes like a miniature volcano; and at the white-flecked waters simmering above the causeway where it dipped before turning towards Hexney.

Billy Ogden had had enough of waiting. He put his head down to meet the wind, and walked along the platform towards the crossing-keeper's cottage. Past the steaming and bubbling of the locomotive, the wind struck full at him. But in two years aboard the *Turakina* on the New Zealand run he had met ten times worse than this. And been battered by far deeper, more furious waters. He was not going to be held back now, this close to his girl, by a few wind-whipped shallows over a road.

Mrs. Dunstall shielded her eyes from a sudden, venomous gust.

Billy said: 'What d'you reckon to it? What's going on up there?'

'All clouded over.' The words were torn away by the wind as she uttered them. 'It wasn't that girl. Not her. I did her an ill turn . . .'

'What *is* it?'

'You ask me,' said Mrs. Dunstall,

'something wicked once got a foothold in there, long ago, and nobody's ever properly dislodged it.'

Two others, a middle-aged man and woman, shuffled their way along behind Billy, reluctant to be left on their own.

'Well, then?' The man could barely raise his head.

'We shouldn't have come,' said his wife. 'We'll never get across there tonight.'

'It was you said you wanted to get back to the house.'

'And we can't.'

'After getting this far — '

'What are they doing to it?' she asked Mrs. Dunstall. 'We got this feeling we oughtn't to have gone away — not this time — this year's something special, and we oughtn't to have left our house to . . . to whatever it is. Best under your own roof, keeping an eye on things.'

'I got a notion she was calling me,' said Billy, trying to separate smoke from lowering cloud above the distant gateway. 'Nigh on to calling me, and me already on my way from Wellington. And then she gave up, all of a sudden, but still I got it strong inside me . . . and I still got it, but not from her, like.'

Mrs. Dunstall said: 'I can't just stay here. Not any longer.'

'If there was a boat — '

'There is.' She waved him across the embankment in front of the engine, towards the curve of the dyke. 'Down there, unless it's been swep' away.'

The farther bank of the dyke was threatening to subside below the water, but this one held firm. A punt was moored to a rickety stake, threatening to go down by the stern as the painter tightened, secured below what was now water level. Billy slithered along the wet, muddy ridge, tried the reliability of the stake, and reached out for the painter. He hauled the punt to the bank.

'You coming with me, then?'

The woman said: 'We should never have come. Should never have got that upset.'

'We've come this far, we'll go the whole way now.'

Mrs. Dunstall crossed the rails. 'I'm coming with you.'

Billy held the punt steady as they

climbed gingerly in.

The man said: 'You've got the strength, lad. I'll navigate. I know the lie of the land — not a cut nor a shallow nor a tuft I don't know. Right?'

'Right.'

They swung out into the channel. The driver and fireman of the train watched them, dark driftwood on the black and frothy waters, and then looked away at the uncertain line of embankment ahead and wondered if it would hold.

Billy paddled feverishly to starboard to hold the boat on course beside the causeway, following the line of the ditch. His coxswain snapped an occasional direction, and a dozen times the wind played vicious jokes to toss him off course; but gradually they drew closer to Hexney. The surface of the water was whipped to an apparent tumult, but it remained shallow over most of its expanse, and only unreasoning panic could lead them into real danger.

All at once the going was easier. They were under the lee of the village, closing in towards the spot where the road emerged from the water and rose to the gateway.

Sparks were sucked up and over the wall. They could hear a faint chanting.

'That cloud . . . Fred, you'd swear there was a mouth, and look — like eyes, aren't they? And . . . no, I don't like it. We should never have — '

'Don't let those old wives' tales get at you. I'm a sight more worried about our thatch being set on fire.'

They bumped in at the side of the hill.

The wind moaned along the wall, and at the gateway joined an eddy of sound from inside, chanting in unison a high-pitched psalm.

The cottages outside the gate were unlit. The arch itself flickered red.

'All that thatch, they must have gone off their heads.'

Mrs. Dunstall let out a little whimper, then bravely took Billy Ogden's arm and said:

'Best we go and see for ourselves, once and for all.'

They walked through the gateway.

The singing faded, but not because

anyone had noticed the newcomers. All heads were turned to look at the gibbet. A cart had been manhandled under it, carrying a bearded man pinioned beneath the dangling noose, with a young woman huddled at his feet.

'That Miss Powys,' said Mrs. Dunstall: 'I knew they meant her no good, I ought never to have . . . '

The singing had quite died. There was no sound other than the sudden crackle as two men hurled armfuls of wood on the fire. Flames lanced out towards the gibbet.

A black silhouette was erect and cold against the glare. 'Do you repent your rejection of the true gods?'

'I have never rejected the truth.'

'You have lived on lies. Drawn from the true magic and denied it. Will you confess and be cleansed by the Great Mistress?'

'I confess to none of your perversities.'

'The Great Mistress of being and non-being loves you. She will smile upon you. Or scourge you. Yours is the choice. Will you now acknowledge — '

'I acknowledge nothing. I do not see you.'

'Will! William Jephson!'

There was a rustle of disquiet, quickly suppressed.

Will Jephson and Leah Morritt sat cross-legged, facing each other, under the blistered remains of Gregory Morritt. Their skin glistened in the firelight. They were wet with impatience, raging to burst out again at the culmination of the rite.

Sarah Jephson, calling his name, emerged from drifting smoke and the shadows of the square, walking in time with the remembered rhythm. She reached the two squatting on the grass and stood above them. Her fingers plucked at the buttons on her jacket. Looking at her husband's body, smeared with sweat and earth, she flinched; but her eyes were tranced, and she sank to her knees and touched him.

'If that's how it must be, you'll find me better than that one.'

He stirred from a coma, blinking at her without recognition.

'I promise,' she said, her voice slurred yet confident. 'I know now, and I promise.'

Two old women cackled out of the shadow. A girl swallowed an uneasy laugh.

The black priest raised his arms.

'Begone, child. This is not as decreed.'

Will Jephson rose to his feet, his belly gashed by bright red stains of lashing flame. Leah put up an arm to drag him down again.

Sarah laughed as none of her friends had ever heard her laugh before, or as her husband had ever heard her laugh. Her head was thrown back, her hair loose, her body cringing yet hugging a new knowledge to itself. Will trod across a burning brand without feeling it, and dug his fingers into her forearms, as if to stop her tearing at her clothes; then slackened his grip.

The priest hurled broken incantations into the broken drift of smoke and flame and ash.

Billy Ogden said: 'No. I don't believe it, I don't believe none of it.'

Carrie Lavater let out a wail of dismay. 'Billy, go back! I didn't send for you, I didn't, honest I didn't. Go back . . . '

'I don't believe it,' said Billy again.

The priest's invocation became a shriek.

And out of the welter of dark and light,

dancing shadows and genuflecting bodies, out of earth and sky and soil and mud, the vast and impossible chimera reared free of the footprints and flowed around the green, a tide of viscous runnels diverging and rejoining, splashing up and over crouched and standing figures, spurting up higher to fall again, to fall in palpitating greed on upturned faces, flowing on over stake and fire and the bloody carcass which sagged from the pillory — feeding without consuming, yet growing each second on what it sucked up, drawing its worshippers into a vast, fetid embrace.

Across the heads of the throng, Caspian implored: 'Don't see it. It has no power if you disbelieve. It can only be what you make it — what *you* make it!'

The mouth of hell leered at him.

It was slobbering fecundity from the sea depths, greed incarnate, mother of all the spawn of fish and beast and man and monster, a million faces and a million appetites all demanding to be sated at once though forever insatiable.

'Tradioun marexil,' intoned the priest,

'fir tru dinxye bnrrudizhye ... O marikeriu, O merikariba ... mordendor, mordendor ...'

Blind copulation, the orgasm of chaos, seed and flesh of the cold-blooded and the hot-blooded running insane into a universe avid for insanity ...

Sea Mother and Earth Mother, threshing in primeval slime before there was sea or earth.

Creator of the joke of evil, most hysterical of all jokes.

We deny you.

Caspian and Bronwen stared together into the manifestation of chaos as it was and wished to be again.

We refuse to see.

An old woman seated outside The Griffin glimpsed her own most feared demon in the shape that licked over her, and yielded up her sobbing vomit.

Leah Morritt writhed under the cloud in an ecstasy that was suddenly barren, as Sarah Jephson lured her husband away with her pale body, and the girls on the green sighed a long sigh.

Hannah Morritt looked into the smoke

of the inferno and saw her own face grimacing back at her, magnified a hundred times as if in a distorting mirror.

It has come only because it was called. Dismiss it.

'What's got into you?' Billy Ogden advanced across the square, seeing only Carrie.

She wrestled with a hissing, insidious promise that coiled around her in a numbing cocoon; and forced herself to make two steps to meet Billy.

'Go!' roared Caspian in his mightiest defiance. 'We will not sustain you.'

The web trembled. A victim fell free, gasping. Arms and legs fought against the viscid threads, and snapped them.

Dark fury boiled in upon Caspian. and met the fury unleashed from the depths of his mind.

Bronwen's mind clung to his.

'They ought to be ashamed.' The man and his wife inched their way incredulously across the square, dodging neighbours with stares, which they took to be the aftermath of a drunken debauch. 'I'd never have believed it.'

'Never,'

The deliquescing face of a giantess yearned foul and lascivious at Caspian. the lips gibbering in longing and then dissolving to a pulp.

You shall not have us.

His nightmare became Bronwen's nightmare, struggled in a last gigantic paroxysm for the souls of both of them, and then shredded away into the tangled locks of a thwarted, spitting, venomous Medusa.

The priest backed away into shadows not of his own creating and not those of his immortal Mistress, crying like a child — or a lost thwarted and suddenly terrified animal.

Mrs, Dunstall said: 'They had my Tommy. They shan't have anyone else.'

Caspian and Bronwen felt a pang of terror worse than any yet. For they understood: saw that, unlike Billy Ogden and the other two who had overturned the balance by simply not believing. Mrs. Dunstall had believed. Knowing or half knowing, sensing. responding to ancient echoes from the village and whatever resonance of horror her son had left shivering above the fen, she had known what she might have to face in Hexney and had come in to face it.

She smiled shakily at them. She heard, as they heard, the malevolent whisper dying away, defeated, into the lost oceans of limbo.

5

The acrid smell of damped-down embers was flurried about the marketplace by the wind, which now blew with unabated zest through the gateway. Half a dozen men swept the cobbles, while the carpenter dismantled his gibbet, looking at each piece in bewilderment as he loaded it on to his cart.

The processions and shufflings about the square last night had obliterated all traces of those footprints, which had been so firmly stamped into the cobbles and the earth. And outside the village wall, high water had churned the prints on the droveway into a sludge of mud and weed.

Billy Ogden stood beside Carrie Lavater on the slope above the priory. The sun was brightening, clouds were being blown away at a great rate. He thought of scudding before such a wind across a bright ocean, and looked out on a scene none too different: mile upon mile of water rolled away to the sharp line of the horizon, concealing dykes and banks and roads.

He said: 'Right, then. What were you doing last night?'

'I don't know.'

'You can't tell me — '

'Honest, Billy, I don't know. It's . . . all gone.'

'And what you said about not sending for me. What did you mean by all that?'

'Billy,' she said, 'I'm glad you're here.'

In The Griffin, Leah Morritt mopped the counter, not because it needed it but because there didn't seem anything else to do. There could only have been one customer last night. Josh Serpell's mug was the only one left on the bar from last night, unwashed. She had no recollection of serving him; or of having been in the taproom at all. It must have been quiet in here for once.

She stopped, leaned on the counter, and stared out of the window.

She remembered. What did she remember? She closed her eyes; opened them again; still saw nothing. There must have been somebody. She had meant it, and somebody had meant it, and there'd been what you might call a blessing on it. A sort of blessing Will Jephson: yes, that was it, surely? She dipped into the pocket of her apron and found a fur tippet. Will Jephson . . .

But she didn't remember him, not really. She tried to see him and see him clearly, and be sure, but it was no use. All she remembered was a devilish heat, and a devilish strength inside her.

Leah put the cloth down. She was quite sure, even this morning, that she was going to have a child.

Will Jephson's? She had no recollection, no idea; and somehow it didn't matter.

Sarah Jephson was in her kitchen, wearing her blue and white cotton dress, with the cuffs pinned well back, and a dark blue apron. When Will came through from the scullery, leaving the door open, she looked past him at a patch of sky, and said:

'Well?'

He shrugged. 'Well, then?'

'You've been looking around.'

'Yes.'

'And it's . . . all over?'

'Over?'

'Whatever it was. Will — it's all over?'

'Oh.' he said. 'Oh, yes, I reckon it is.' He shook his head and looked back, up at the sky as if a racing cloud might tell him something. 'Yes, I reckon it must be.'

She stood across his path and he kissed her, his mouth staying on hers for longer than usual. When he drew away he grinned awkwardly, not knowing quite what to make of her; but she knew he liked the feel of her, he'd liked it last night and he'd like it again, when she let him. And she wasn't going to starve him.

When he passed her she turned ever so slightly to watch him go, her eyes shrewder and less forgetful than his.

Ash settled in a fine layer on the window ledge of The Griffin.

'A dreadful thing,' said Constable Rylot.

He stood by the remains of the bonfire and prodded a seared bone with his foot.

'You remember, then?' said Caspian.

'Poor Gregory. A sorry ending to it all,

362

that. You wouldn't know him, I don't suppose, sir — miss?'

'I remember him,' said Bronwen defiantly.

'Cast quite a gloom on things, that did, him falling into the fire like that.'

'Falling . . . ?'

'Must have had a lot more'n was good for him. Not like him to go at it like that, but him being a bit moody, and then all that trouble with his wife and her showing herself off with others, I suppose it all went to his head.'

By the churchyard wall Mrs. Morritt, already shrouded in black, waited for Mrs. Lavater and Mrs. Rylot to catch up with her. Solemnly her friends ranged themselves one on either side of her, and walked up the path to the porch, making plans in hushed voices.

Bronwen said: 'But he couldn't just have fallen, and been left to . . . to . . . '

'It was late, miss. Lots of folks had gone to bed, and he was helping to stamp the fire out, and it blazed up quicker than anyone would ha' thought — too fierce for any of 'em to get near him.'

Was that all it had been, then: a village romp, interpreted or misinterpreted in different ways by different participants; a village fête, harmless but for an unfortunate accident to one local man who would be mourned for a while, talked about spasmodically for a while, and then relegated to the past?

Caspian led Bronwen away.

She said: 'But surely there'll have to be an inquest. And we'll have to report what really happened.'

'What *really* happened, so far as the rest of them were concerned?'

'We saw — '

'We know what we saw, and we remember what they saw. But the rest of them don't. Look at them.'

Two women crossed the square, a man with a twelve-bore over his shoulder trudged towards the gateway. They glanced incuriously at the strangers — foreigners — as they passed. They were blank and indifferent, not with the previous days' stupor but with the unknowing, uncommunicative Hexney manner comfortably settled upon them.

Bronwen said: 'Mrs. Dunstall saw.'

'Did she? I don't know how much she assimilated in detail. And even three of us, testifying against the actual inhabitants — can you imagine what impression we'd make at a coroner's inquest? A whole community of sober, unimaginative villagers telling the straightforward story of a commonplace accident — and then three of us coming out with the most fantastic nightmare the court will ever have heard. Whose evidence will carry the day?'

They turned back towards the inn. It was surely time to pack and be gone; and this time to be sure of not returning.

But if it comes again . . . if the rector and the others slink away again, handing over the place . . . '

'Not in this century. Or so its servant proclaimed. And when it does return, perhaps conditions will be unsuitable. Next time it may not be Hexney. There are other villages with ancient festivals ready to be restored to their original purpose: furry dances the running of horn dancers and the battle between black and white, the boggans playing house against house and burning their chosen Fool . . . old rituals drained of evil but ready to be replenished. And worse.'

'Worse?'

'More civilized centres, ready for subtler corruption. More dangerous in the end than the outbreaks of minor epidemics in isolated villages. City dabblers too clever for their own good but too ignorant to know what they're concocting. Perhaps even whole nations waiting to be spurred into mindless fury.'

'And we — we two, after what we have learnt . . . or tried to learn . . . ?'

'We must be ready.'

We must be together. Always.

Aloud he said: 'Will you marry me?'

'I thought we were already married. Or have you tired of the woman you've discovered me to be, and fancy trying another one?'

'I'm asking you on human terms. So that I have both; and you have both; and we have each other, which will be one.' Caspian laughed. 'And it will be as well to regularize our place in society — save a deal of trouble in the end.'

And we shall continue to explore . . . to love . . .

His mind was against hers, his lips on hers; he was everywhere.

'Is there so much more we have to learn?' she breathed.

'So much,' he said. 'A lifetime of it.'

THE END